Friendship
and
Afterwards

CW01551715

Friendship
and
Afterwards

DANIEL GOTHARD

Copyright ©

This first edition published in Great Britain in 2014 by
Yolk Publishing Limited

ISBN 978-1-910130-01-8

Available from www.yolkpublishing.co.uk
All major online retailers and available to order through all UK bookshops

Or contact:

Books
Yolk Publishing Limited
145-157 St John Street
London
EC1V 4PW

books@yolkpublishing.co.uk
www.yolkpublishing.co.uk

Printed in the UK by Yolk Publishing Ltd
Yolk's policy is to use papers that are natural, renewable and recyclable products and
made from wood grown in sustainable forests wherever possible

This book is dedicated to my wife Zoe
and our children Jasmine, Joe and Natty.

I would like to pay special thanks and acknowledge
the huge amount of support and encouragement I have received
over the years: Ann Gothard, Clare and Pradeep Shakya,
Patricia Freeman, Ben Hamilton, Louise Dean, Peter Hamilton,
the late Peter Preston, Peter Pegnall, Tricia Wastvedt,
Tessa Hadley, Tom Chalmers, Guy Mankowski
Mark J Mayes and Hayley Webster.

I am extremely grateful to James Hobbs and Carla Greco
of Yolk Publishing for taking a chance on me as
their first signed author and for all their hard work.
This book would never have succeeded without the brilliant
editorial work of my great friend Shane Garrigan.
He has been an invaluable source of endless patience
and wisdom over many years.

Hemingway said you write for the one you love, and I do.
This story is for my wife.

Finally I would like to acknowledge the work of Richard Yates.
His novels and short stories
have made me a much better writer.

David

David had expected shouting, screaming even. He had expected Sarah to throw something at him. She was drinking tea when he told her he was leaving, ending their eight years together, that he had fallen in love with someone else and out of love with her. All that came his way was a calm request: Sarah wanted his house keys, and him out of the house that day.

She wanted a clean break. A clean break. As if there could ever be such a thing when love has the energy crushed out of it. They had had sex the night before, the first intimacy of any kind between them in a long time, and something about the complete lack of connection, of passion, had acted as the catalyst for that following day being the one for his 'big news'.

After the initial request for the keys, she asked David again and again to hand them over. He knew he was being churlish in withholding the damn things, but he felt it was his right to keep them – in the short term at the very least. What's the rush, he thought, he was still paying half the mortgage and the utility bills. Didn't that entitle him to a key? She could change the locks any day, but his name was on the deeds. He had some rights of free access and exit, he guessed.

He avoided giving them to her because it meant the end. He changed the subject each time, giving an acknowledging nod of the head when she pushed him to hand them over, and making some excuse or other about needing to collect the last of his possessions. There was so much to organise, he said; they shouldn't be hasty. He knew he was appearing to be flippant about many things in the initial period of separation. He ignored the pain in her eyes – they looked red and sore – and the way she continually scratched her arm and followed him around the house, looking over his shoulder when he took a novel from the bookshelves or selected a CD. They even disagreed about who bought the Roy Lichtenstein reproduction postcard on the fridge door.

David wanted to pretend everything was normal. He was pushing the pain of the open wound into a compartment in his mind – 'File that for later' – and dealing only with the immediate business of the everyday. He was a marketing manager for a recycled products business and he was attempting to deal with the break-up as he would a new client; the territory was unknown and he would obviously be nervous at first. But this was the start of life after her. He hadn't imagined he would ever be with anyone else and he occasionally stopped and wondered who was this person inside him destroying an entire history and beginning an existential makeover?

Things didn't need to be chaotic and full of re-criminations. They could split amicably.

He spent his time at work pretending he liked his job. He drank endless cups of coffee with the odd cigarette throughout the day and made appointments out of the office whenever he could. He made certain he was looking at some papers when his boss was in close proximity: he had read an article stating there was an automatic presumption of assiduous behaviour when a person was holding a piece of paper.

He had always wanted to sell their house and return to Florence, where they had travelled to five years before, and sit by the River Arno, sketching and watching her profile in the sunshine. He would have been happy to live and die slowly, existing simply in the hills outside the city, perhaps buried next to her eventually in the graveyard of the small church they had found: Santa Maria something or the other…

Had he ever told her about that dream? Would she have thought him mad or feckless, and perhaps ended the relationship herself?

Instead he had become a conventional desk-jock-ey, telling himself, when he first got the job, it was cool to work with recycled goods; it was an ethical career that would contribute to saving the planet. But he was pretending he knew what he was doing with the marketing of these expensive and unattractive recycled things. What was marketing anyway – making up lies about items you don't really like, need or want? Was it normal to work day after day without a clue?

The break-up can be treated as normal, he thought. We've come to an end, people do all the time, and what I'm doing couldn't really be thought of as callous. I am still paying half of everything and I'm leaving the house.

He was a good person. He reminded himself of that in his head throughout the days after he said he was leaving Sarah. He held doors open for people. He made colleagues tea or coffee. He had to be good, otherwise everything he had done could be seen as wrong, his entire existence tainted, and he would be nowhere, a loser.

Surely he had done enough good deeds in the world, even at such a young age of twenty-nine, to be given a free pass on leaving a relationship because he had fallen out of love with one person and in love with another?

He had kept his mother together mentally and emotionally when his father left them, helping her keep the family home going by ditching his university education and getting a job to pay her mortgage. And later, providing an alibi for his brother when he drunkenly wrote off a second car in twelve months, by saying he was driving the car instead. He had always tried to do his best in all things – the things people expected him to do – to earn his way in life, to be in the right place at the right time.

Now he was doing the completely unexpected and unwanted and he knew there was no good way of leaving – that was just a folly. The act of leaving, of destruction, could never be padded and cosy. There would always be words and stares, memories that scarred the soul and dreams that recurred and haunted the person who ruined everything.

A lot of David's possessions were stored in boxes in the recently boarded and insulated loft. They had talked about a full conversion in the future; a decision about having four children had progressed to the subject of needing more space.

He made certain most of his 'visit time' in the first week of separation was spent sitting alone in the musty, humid space above their bedroom, slowly, painfully weighing up the pros and cons of various LPs, books and items of complete disinterest, which he felt ridiculous for having bothered storing in the first place. A pair of re-whitened Dunlop tennis pumps, hardened by mud and damp, were a memory of his early attempts to impress Sarah with his athletic abilities. He watched thin shafts of sunlight illuminate motes of dust, daydreaming for a moment, letting his hands run back and forth through the light. Then he looked through a tiny crack in the brickwork that faced on to the back garden. There he saw the half-finished beds he had promised to create. 'I'll be like a modern version of Capability Brown,' he had told Sarah when they moved in to the house.

What a joyless experience that had proved to be: back-breaking Saturday and Sunday morning work. They used to make love at the weekends, but now it was all about the vacuum cleaning and mowing the lawn.

His eyes moved to the bowing whirly dryer he

had convinced Sarah didn't need embedding with a concrete foundation. Half-finished this-and-thats in the relationship filled his head: the bathroom wall on which mildew kept re-appearing – he had promised he would find a way to solve that problem; the case of the food cupboard door hinge which persistently slipped to one side when you opened and closed it – he had used some newspaper to wedge it straight. Was he only capable of fifty percent? Would this separation mean him living in the loft, eyeing the staircase and hallway from above to see when he could come down to eat, wash, use the loo and leave for work, half in and half out of the house?

David sat next to the water tank, listening to Sarah's muffled voice on the telephone two floors below. He couldn't hear what she was saying, but he guessed she might be complaining to a friend or relative about his continued presence. He looked at various photographs: weddings, days out, and the Italian holiday that had meant so much to him.

They had started that trip abroad – their first together – in Pisa, managing to locate a bed and breakfast villa just yards away from the Leaning Tower.

David looked at a shot of the two of them taken by some obliging local, their arms around each other, grinning like young lovers do, with the Tower behind them. David had been wearing the US Varsity imitation jacket he had bought specifically for the holiday, brand new then, stained, dusty and badly folded at the foot of the box of photographs he was looking through now.

He studied his younger face in the Tower photo. He looked genuinely happy to be there, happy to be with her. How had that evaporated? Was his soul so wretched he couldn't hold on to a deep feeling, a sense of something good in his life? He could analyse himself in an amateurish fashion and conclude, as he had done hundreds of times before, that his childhood was to blame for all the bad thoughts, feelings and actions in his burgeoning adult life. But that was bullshit and he knew it. He was fond of Corinthians 1:13 in the New Testament, not because he was a Believer (although he re-read the extract regularly), just as a memory from enforced visits to Sunday school. He agreed with the idea of putting away Childish Things. He was at fault in this separation. He was the one leaving.

The Leaning Tower photo reminded him how young they had been when they got together: twenty-years old, both students at university, and new to life away from the confines of family, elated by falling in love for the first time.

Although his hair was cropped short in the photo, he knew he was thinner on top now; his scalp had started to burn in the summer months. A widow's peak had begun to develop over the last couple of years. He wondered whether his hair loss might eventually render him unattractive to Alison. But that was ridiculous, wasn't it?

He remembered he was supposed to call Alison that morning to let her know when he would be seeing her later. She preferred calls to text messages. She said it was because she loved hearing his voice and it showed more effort on his part. 'It makes my day to see your name on caller ID. I love that you care so much. You're so lovely,' she said.

The loft search and rescue was taking for ever. He couldn't exhaust all remaining signs of 'good will' with Sarah by coming and going over the same ground.

Sarah said he needed to take what ever he wanted from the loft on this visit and she would throw the rest away with the rubbish collection later in the week.

She was going back to Kent to visit her parents at the weekend and wanted him to 'finish your business of leaving'.

Earlier that day, when he arrived and she made him a cup of tea, he felt a rush of desperate relief at such a small gesture of kindness from her, half expecting her to pour the beverage over his head when it was made. They exchanged a few excruciating formal words, neither of them able to maintain eye contact, like strangers at a bus stop – How's work? How are you sleeping? – while sipping their drinks. Then she left him alone for a moment, collected some papers – a large pile – opened the recycling bin and shoved, pushed and generally forced them in. Then she went to the bathroom.

He was curious to know what could have possibly annoyed her so much about those particular papers, or was it just being near him that made her tense?

He looked over his shoulder and listened out for her. He put his tea down and opened the bin. He could see half an image – a wedding dress – and knew immediately what the stash was. His body responded with a chill down his spine and a drop in his stomach. She had just ditched her wedding file in front of him. A fuck you, fuck you and fuck you again to him. She had probably gone to the bathroom to allow him time to look in the bin and realise how dead he was to her now.

The wedding file had been a source of hard work and pride. It represented three and a half months of preparations: visits to civil ceremony locations; appointments with registrars, event-car companies and marquee owners; and the secretive collection of wedding dress images, which were stored in a re-sealable envelope that he had promised not to look into, and hadn't. They had made up a guest list and decided on the right kind of invitation card. Three and a half months. And for two months of that time he had been in love with, although as he kept telling himself, not actually cheating with, someone else.

Sarah had gone quiet downstairs. He looked at his mobile phone. He had been in the loft for nearly two hours. He must call Alison soon; he couldn't screw up two relationships in one fell swoop. It was a difficult job being a new boyfriend to someone while extricating himself from another person, and not being an arsehole in the process. He looked down from the loft hatch at the recently decorated hall, stairs and landing walls. They had decided on a terracotta hue and used sponges for a 'distressed' look. The job had taken much longer than he thought it would and he had never really liked the colour much. They had bought a new mirror for the hallway too – a faux-gothic frame that always made him think of Hammer Horror films when he arrived home. He knew he would miss the house; paint and mirrors could always be changed.

'Are you going to be much longer? I need to go out soon,' Sarah called up to him, at the foot of the loft ladder. He nearly fell sideways with surprise.

'No, no. Problem is, it's such a mess. Can I come back again and finish the job, maybe tomorrow? Or I could try and get it done now and let myself out?'

A moment's silence followed down below.

'No, that doesn't work for me. I want to be here when you are. I don't feel comfortable letting you wander in and out. It's not fair to put me under any more pressure. Please finish what you're doing now and perhaps we can talk later about a quicker visit tomorrow. All right?' she said.

What he wanted to happen next was to find himself walking down the ladder, stopping a few feet away from her and saying, 'Actually, no, that's not all right at all. I understand you're angry and upset. I completely get that. But I think we can safely assume I won't empty the contents of the house into my Nissan Micra. I'll only take what I'm sure is mine now and leave the rest to consult with you on later. That's my version of all right. I think we need to try and have a bit of separation between feelings and pragmatism, don't you? You want me out as quickly as possible and the only way for me to achieve that is to have the time to achieve it.'

But what he actually said in reply to her was, 'Okay, I'll be right down.'

He wobbled down the ladder carrying two small-ish boxes, aware of her watching him all the way. I bet she would love me to fall and break my neck, he thought, but then he caught sight of the look on her face, and it seemed to be full of anguish. He tried to smile at her reassuringly, but the smile turned into what felt more like a wince.

'I'll call you later, then,' he said, as he reached the front door.

'If you want, that's fine. I might be out, so call my mobile,' she replied, then went into the lounge and shut the door. He let himself out, put the boxes into the boot of his car and slammed it shut.

Surely I can do better than this, he thought. Surely I can make things end better?

He didn't want to phone Alison in the car right outside the front door and window of his ex-home. Sarah might be just on the other side of the net curtain, like a spectre, watching him, tuned in to the frequency of his voice after so many years together, or able to read his lips.

He drove away, around a corner and pulled into the kerbside.

'Hi, it's… well, you know who it is. How are you this morning?'

'It's almost afternoon. I nearly called you a few times to find out what you were up to,' Alison said. She sounded annoyed.

'I've been stuck in a loft for hours, wading through the debris of the past decade. Most of my LPs are warped from the heat and damp, my books are crinkled too, and it was all just unbelievably depressing.'

'Did Sarah make things hard for you?'

Hearing Alison use Sarah's name always surprised David. Ridiculous though it was, he wanted to imagine they were of different worlds and completely unaware of each other, but they did know each other, by name and face. They had spent an odd day together as part of a group of six people just a short while before.

David, his best friend, Ben, and mutual friend Richard had decided the previous year to set up a film production company and begin by concentrating on short films. Ben was the screenwriter, Richard the director and David had taken on the job of producer.

They shot their first film with a handheld digital video camera. The set was built in the flat Ben shared with Richard and Richard's girlfriend, Kate.

It was a one-actor film and the actor was Alison.

She and David worked together, and over various coffee breaks and lunches she had told him of her drama school days and her decision to 'get a real job' after countless rejections.

'So it's a short film, no budget, no frills, maybe a sandwich and cup of tea, shot in one day. How does that sound?' David had said to Alison.

She had laughed and said yes. She had touched his arm in a way that filled him with sexual energy. He spent the rest of the day thinking about her hand:

the shape of it; the feeling against his arm. That was the day he started to think of her as not just a lovely co-worker but as something else entirely different.

The storyline of the script was Alison's character, a medical student, giving a statement to the police about a hand she amputated from a stranger, a homeless man. The statement was full of Kafkaesque allusion to secrecy and conspiracy. The medical student never revealed why she chose the victim, why she wanted the hand, or what she intended to do with the severed body part. During the interview she held the neatly sliced hand, giving a detailed description of how she carried out the amputation, and allowed by the interviewer to paint the nails – David borrowed the fake hand from a department store mannequin. Alison's character punctuated her statement with looks, smiles and nods to one side as if there were someone coaching her in what to say and how to say it.

The video shoot was a paradoxical day for David. For a long time, he had been focusing on arranging a film, a real film, something the three 'production company' members could call their own and use as a calling card to obtain a real budget with real actors so they could produce polished work for short-film festivals. He hadn't conceived the shoot as a ruse to ingratiate himself with Alison, especially with Sarah in the room, but as the day wore on he became aware of how much he liked the way Alison spoke, how she smiled, the way she caressed the severed hand. He liked everything about her. As that realisation took hold of his senses like a narcotic, another part of his personality began to compensate, as if it felt he was a traitor to the very cause of love itself.

He deliberately diverted his attention to Sarah at inappropriate moments, such as breaks between set-ups when he, Richard, Ben and Alison were discussing a particular script idea or brainstorming other ways to place emphasis on words or phrases.

'What do you think, Sarah?' David said on a few occasions when it was obvious to everyone else in the flat that Sarah and Kate's opinions, valid or not, should perhaps come second to the director, writer, producer and actor.

As the group watched the unedited footage playback at the end of the day, David felt happy with the authenticity of the performance and, what he perceived, depth of the script. He had attended a short-film course at the National Film School some months before, and the central ideas he had come away with relating to the type of low-to-no budget filmmaking he was involved with were Interesting and Memorable.

He also felt gripped at the throat by guilt having Alison and Sarah so near each other. Alison had a boyfriend at that time and made a couple of sarcastic references about him to Sarah and Kate, but even those didn't prevent a build-up of sweat under David's armpits. He half expected Alison to say to Sarah, 'Of course, I won't be with that loser for much longer, because I'm going to steal your boyfriend, okay?'

The drive home after the video shoot was quiet and strained by unspoken tension, not because of any arguments but because he was living a lie now: walking, talking and breathing lies, damned lies.

He spent a few minutes running through a set of potentially stress-inducing scenarios in his head; reasons he could produce for his silence, if Sarah asked: pressure at work; planning the wedding and jitters about getting the Big Day right; fatigue after a long day out. He forced his mind to begin the process of convincing himself that perhaps, just perhaps, there was no genuine reason to feel the weight of guilt he was feeling about such an innocuous meeting between the two women. Nothing had happened between him and Alison, and, probably, nothing would ever happen. He pulled the car into the space outside their house and was about to get out.

'You never told me Alison was so pretty,' Sarah said.

Sarah

When David announced he was leaving, he had stood in front of the lounge fireplace to tell Sarah and, for some reason, her first thought was that he looked like a man telling his wife he was 'off to war'. Sarah cried and asked him to stay. It was a kneejerk reaction, something she found herself saying without having the time or mental energy to think through what that would mean. He wanted to leave, so why would he suddenly say, 'Oh, all right then, I'll stay.' And why would she want him to stay after treating her with such contempt?

He had drawn the departure announcement out over that previous weekend.

Friday evening was full of silences – words unspoken on a subject she could see was burning a hole through him. She thought he might want to explain why he had been making so many withdrawals from their joint bank account. She was planning to ask him about that shortly. Or perhaps he wanted to say he was leaving his job. She knew he hated it, and who could blame him: he wanted to be an artist, and he was good.

Saturday was busy with food shopping in the morning, seeing her parents for lunch – they were passing through on a trip to see old friends in the north – and going into town in the evening to watch a film.

Sunday was just plain quiet, a difficult state for her to comprehend or put into words when she thought through their last hours as a couple; attempting to slow-motion the last part of their relationship in mostly failed attempts to analyse why and when things had finally collapsed. She spoke a lot about that last weekend to her closest friends and family later on.

David had made her a cup of tea and brought it to her in bed, a regular gesture of kindness, which if she were being honest, she had come to expect.

He left the room quickly – he usually sat on the bed with his cup of tea and chatted – and she remembered when they first moved into the house and made love throughout the week, and always at the weekend. But that was then, and now weekends were all about seeing friends and family, watching films or gigs, or the planning and implementation of home improvements.

As Sarah looked back over the lead-up to his departure, she realised they had slowly constructed a life where they didn't really talk to each other about anything other than what would, could or might happen next. Was that what other couples did when they had nothing real to say to each other? Weren't there causes to find and people in need around the country, the world – something that could have enriched their lives by becoming a part of?

They had joined a local anti-hunt group once, but

David eventually talked her out of demonstrating and in to leaving the group as he said they were being hypocrites by eating meat while trying to stop animals being killed. He said the same thing on another occasion when she signed an anti-vivisection petition.

Did her experience of his methods in living mean she should have had some kind of foreknowledge that he would be leaving? Didn't she know him so well that she should have seen, or felt, that he was planning a big move? She guessed, sitting alone, partially drunk, on the second night after he left, that she had been blinded by the wedding plans. She assumed he was as mentally tied up in knots of anxiety and excitement as she was. But no, the bastard was planning to leave her at the same time as he was opining on civil ceremony locations and the invitation designs. He seemed so interested in her wedding file, leafing through the pages and opening discussions on the order of the day: photographs with family and friends; setting a website address for music suggestions; and whether to have an open bar, or place wine and water on each table and let the guests pay themselves to reduce overheads.

Jesus, he really was a complete bastard, a liar, a soulless pig. She was well rid of him. True enough it hurt to be left alone after so many years as a couple. The act of being together was an addictive habit, but she could beat that addiction, perhaps by becoming addicted to someone else, and move on. She was young and practical, and he would soon miss her, probably knocking on her door in a few weeks or months, begging her to take him back. And that would be her moment.

At least they hadn't spent any wedding money yet. Thank god she wasn't jilted on the day itself. He humiliated her by leaving, but being left alone in front of a grimacing, sweating registrar, who had probably overseen many jiltings, surrounded by everyone you know – whispered conversations of sympathy, shuffling feet and embarrassed coughs – would have smashed her into a catatonic hell.

Sarah suggested they make a real effort to finish some work in the back garden on that last, oblivious day. It bothered her to watch weekend after weekend slip by as they approached autumn without the garden features being completed. It seemed to signify a gremlin in their way of life, the opposite of the wedding planning, which was fervent and active, alive and full of order. After he said he was going, she wanted to ignore the flora and fauna, let it all grow into a wilderness and take over, like a Nature version of Miss Havisham.

He seemed less than enthusiastic about the garden work, but that was normal. He couldn't be called habitually lazy, just occasionally indolent when he found a task so boring and inconsequential that he could barely think of actually participating in it.

Her father offered to team up with David for an hour or two the previous day after lunch, cut the grass and put in some bedding plants.

That approach seemed to annoy David, although he tried to hide it by joking with her father about not wanting to rush a work of art. He had a plan for a Piet Mondrian-inspired design: vivid colours and blank shapes that would make looking out of the windows a magical experience. All lies.

'You up for the domesticity push today?' Sarah shouted from the bathroom, after her shower. No reply came back.

She found him downstairs holding his mobile phone, his face deadly serious, finishing a text. He put it back into his pocket as if it were something he wanted to keep out of sight, maintaining eye contact with her.

'You all right?' he asked.

'I am. Are you?'

'Sure. I'll make a start on the grass.'

She should have known at that very moment he was covered in deceit and lies. The way he leapt to his feet, smiling as he passed by her and stroked her shoulder. He had been inflated, transformed into a different person by something or someone else. Transformed by her – by that fucking Alison bitch.

They worked for a few hours, stopping every so often to confer on the placing of the colours and whether they needed to dig deeper here or there. David's mobile phone beeped with new messages a few times. He wiped his forehead each time, removed his gloves and read the texts.

'Important news?' Sarah said after the third message.

'Just Ben, blathering on about the editing,' he replied.

He looked her in the eyes and lied through his smiling teeth. He may as well have slapped her with his gloves and whacked her over the head with his spade too.

Sarah hadn't decided whether or not to be angry with Ben yet. She liked him, always had, and she had no idea how complicit, or not, he had been in the Alison deception.

She always enjoyed seeing Ben. He made her laugh – really laugh. In fact they had shared a strange moment a couple of months before, a moment when she had questioned her future with David.

The three of them – Ben was often between girlfriends – had been out for an evening. They had a few drinks in a pub and then decided to have a meal in a local pie restaurant. At one point during the meal, Sarah quizzed Ben on his use of the word beatific. Ben insisted its meaning was based on the ideas of the Beat Poets; he was a big Kerouac, Burroughs and Ginsberg fan.

'Its origins are in the rhythm of life, the various beats of the feelings you get when witnessing different art forms or artistic inspiration,' he said.

'What? It means blissful, bestowing happiness. You're joking, right?' she said. She was a bit tipsy and certain he would grin any second and admit he was deliberately being a fake, winding her up.

'No it doesn't, that's nonsense,' Ben said, and exhaled from the corner of his mouth in frustration..

They continued to argue the pointless point until David asked if anyone wanted another drink and left them in annoyed silence. That moment could have opened a raw fissure in their usually light conversation/ jokey relationship. But something about the intensity of the conversation, the way Ben had tried so long and hard to convince her he was right, how important her approbation seemed to be to him, reanimated a part of her mind that used to buzz with interest in subjects and ideas she hadn't thought about, let alone talked through, since university days.

Ben was all about ideas and projects: photography; writing poetry and prose; travelling abroad to paint. He was a doer.

The evenings with Ben usually ended after food and one or two more drinks in the pub, and then he would sleep in their spare bedroom. But on this particular night, as they walked home, Sarah suggested they join a nightclub queue.

'I really want to dance,' she said.

David pulled his usual bored face, but the look on Ben's face was the complete opposite. It seemed like the exact thing he had wanted to happen too.

The club was hot, crowded and loud, and Sarah couldn't have been any happier.

'I might not stay,' David shouted in her ear.

'What?' she replied.

'I'm really tired. I think I might go home, unless you want me to stay?'

'No, that's fine. I'll walk back with Ben. See you later.'

David kissed her on the cheek, waved to Ben and walked out.

Ben had managed to get to and from the bar with their drinks reasonably quickly, and they sat at a table watching other people dance.

'Shall we?' Ben said, his breath and lips brushing Sarah's ear.

She looked at him with a frowning smile. He smiled back, wriggled an upper-body dance move in his chair and pointed to the floor. She nodded and they stood up together.

At first she felt limited by inhibition in the way she moved. Even with the ease that came from alcohol, she fell back into her usual sway-dance style – David had rudely described it as like watching someone practice skiing while standing virtually still. That was typical of his sense of humour, making fun of other people's faults to show how clever he was.

Even though she often found herself laughing along with him, especially after a few drinks, Sarah had always disliked such a cruel streak in her partner. She put it down to the chip he carried on his shoulder from never having achieved as much as he felt he should after attending university, then living every day after, regretting yet never admitting it or talking about it to anyone, even his closest friend or partner.

As she watched Ben move – he seemed to her to be a very good dancer – she felt her body free itself and go with the pulse of the music.

Then their eyes locked and they danced together, close and in time, watching only each other as if the whole floor was theirs.

Sarah momentarily thought of Uma Thurman and John Travolta at the beginning of their dance in Pulp Fiction, but then she lost control of her thoughts and just revelled in her emotional responses, perhaps the messages in Ben's eyes.

And then she felt beatific.

Alison

Alison Latimer had always wanted to be an actress. In the early part of her childhood she developed the commonplace ideas of saving animals and looking after the infirm, but acting became the thing in her life and she felt as if she would never be able to shake it, or want to. Ever since she saw a West End production of Uncle Vanya with her parents when she was eleven, she wanted to live in other worlds, in other characters' skins, and say the most beautiful and powerful dialogue.

She enjoyed films and television, and would almost certainly have said yes to virtually any part in a movie or series, but the theatre was the place she felt she belonged.

She listened intently as her secondary school drama teacher, Miss Peters, told her of the near-certain failure of ambition that came with having the acting bug.

'I went to RADA and was in the same graduating class as Marianne Jean-Baptiste. She got in with Mike

Leigh and was an Oscar and Golden Globe nominee, and I spent six years trying and failing to get small parts on soap operas and adverts,' Miss Peters said. 'It's a crazy, horrible business, but if it's what you feel in your bones, then have a go.' She smiled weakly.

Alison wanted to ask her why she was teaching drama if she didn't believe in its possibilities but instead smiled back.

Alison finished her compulsory education and made five applications to drama schools, including RADA. Her father was obviously unhappy his daughter wasn't seeking out what he called 'real vocational courses' but mostly kept his opinions to himself.

After interviews and three rejections, Alison received an offer of a place at the Guildhall School of Music and Drama. As she re-read the offer letter over and over, she was sure it was a sign that she would be like Marianne Jean-Baptiste, not Miss Peters, and her talents would shine through her performances and her acting future was secured.

Drama school wasn't like Miss Peters' classes or the school productions she had starred in. Alison found the theoretical perspectives hard to grasp: Lee Strasberg's method style and its adherence to large parts of Stanislavski's The System made her crave simplicity. She understood the ideas of linking real emotions and experiences to performance, the depth an actor could find in his or her own life and how that could inform delivery of dialogue, phrasing, facial expressions and body language. That seemed easy to understand, but the teaching of the theory, the stopping and starting, the re-thinking of each sentence in each scene made her head throb by the end of the working day.

There was one very bright light in the drama school that year of enrollment called Nicholas Adams. He seemed to have been ready-made as an actor before joining the course, equipped with the leading-man package: good looks – better than good in fact, he was a beautiful-looking man; tremendous and immediately obvious abilities as an actor that made her both envious and enchanted; and an empathetic kindness for her when ever they chatted after classes about technique, iambic pentameters or those pesky theories of personality-immersion.

'So your grandfather worked for David Lean and your dad with Steven Spielberg?' Alison asked Nicholas over a third glass of wine one evening. She was still awestruck, as if he was a star already, just by association with the Greats of film. They had been a couple for a few weeks and she was enjoying every moment of finding out new things about him.

'Yep. They were both assistant directors, leaders of huge crews, loyal to those guys.'

'But you didn't want to go into directing?'

'No, being behind the camera never seemed to be where the real action, the art was. I visited a few sets, but I was always watching the actors, the details in their performances. You see, my mother was an actor, is an actor, an amateur really, but great in her own way…local am dram things. I used to go to all her rehearsals, watch her put on her make-up and costumes, practice her lines, her vocal exercises. I looked at her eyes, her mouth, the way she became different people for each play and part, as if she was capable of completely transforming. I wanted to do what she did. It seemed like the only way to really live, by living through many other lives. Does that make any sense?'

Nicholas laughed at himself. He held up his wine glass and made a face of self-mocking as if the alcohol had pickled his brain already. Alison laughed too and fell deeper in love with him.

'It makes perfect sense to me. That's how I feel too.'

'I mean, I do want to direct eventually, in the theatre mainly, as well as act. I want to do what Olivier did, become the ultimate man of words and action. He was amazing: a Hollywood star, the personification of a Shakespearean actor and the founder and director of the National Theatre. I've read everything I can about his life.'

When Alison watched Nicholas deliver a quiet soliloquy or leap from a staircase and project his lines with angry energy perfectly to the furthest reaches of the rehearsal rooms, acting did seem to make sense – because of Nicholas. He was student and teacher.

Inevitably, an actor with his charisma, looks and talent, Nicholas attracted other actors too, and there was one particular actor who made it obvious she wanted to replace Alison.

Jane Pritchard was young and beautiful and talented, but she let it be known in idle canteen chatter that she had always known looks and ability would never be enough. Jane was only too happy to talk about herself and her aspirations, some of which Alison heard directly, other bits were added on by envious friends. She had come to drama school with two very specific goals: learn how to be the best she could be as an actor; and then find a partner to learn from and share the limelight with, like Richard Burton and Elizabeth Taylor or Brad Pitt and Angelina Jolie – create a new golden couple who 'come up' together and create enough buzz to get them both work after drama school, the way Ralph Fiennes and Alex Kingston did after they left RADA. Schindler's List and ER weren't too shabby.

Jane had a plan for success; she would never end up waitressing or taking temporary office jobs between auditions. The plan was something she had discussed in fine detail with her mother, who was not so much a willing accomplice but more the designer of the plan. Her mother failed as a novelist and painter herself, and always wanted to be part of an arts family. Her maternal grandmother had been a member of the 'Bloomsbury Group' and she had grown up feeling cheated by her own parents' lack of creativity. She married Jane's father partly due to the fact that he was, at the time they met, a relatively successful poet. She thought she might be destined to be his muse, but he became more interested in writing books of academic theory as the years passed by. So the second her child showed dramatic inclination she rushed her to Saturday morning acting classes.

Jane let it be known she admired Nicholas, thought he was in a class of his own in the school, and she enraged Alison by working so hard to make Nicholas laugh, which he often did around her.

Eventually an audition notice was placed for a production of Romeo and Juliet.

Jane guessed, aloud, Nicholas was a shoo-in for Romeo, and she would kill to be his Juliet. And all the time, all through the lead-up to the auditions, Alison could see the looks of desire, the blatant cupidity, for her lover in Jane Pritchard's green eyes.

Alison and Nicholas read the play aloud to each other, taking the greatest care over the major scenes. Alison felt the constant tremor of excitement at the thought of becoming Juliet with the love in her soul for Nicholas, but also the dread of a recurring premonition of losing him each time she spoke Juliet's last words: '...there rust, and let me die.'

Alison asked for Nicholas's guidance on the best way to find Juliet inside herself.

'Think of your greatest need and desire, then imagine you are forbidden to ever have it, that you may be killed if you try and take it,' he said. Alison didn't have to imagine too hard to find that sense of emotional depravation. She felt to lose Nicholas would be worse than death for her.

On the day of the audition for the part of Juliet, Alison had the beginnings of a cold. She had the constant trickle and taste of phlegm in her throat, her voice was becoming husky and her forehead felt hot.

'Typical, the first time I'm up for a really important part and I get a virus,' she said to Nicholas, who was sitting opposite her, eating toast and pulling a deeply sympathetic face. They had left early for the audition and stopped at a café on the way for breakfast. 'I thought the only virus I had to worry about in this audition was bloody Jane Pritchard.'

Nicholas laughed and sipped his tea. He stroked her hand.

'You'll knock them dead,' he said.

Alison smiled, rolled her eyes in mock frustration and cracked the foil on a paracetamol blister pack. She took two, looked at her watch to decide whether she had time for some ibuprofen too before the audition began, and then ate some of her bagel and cream cheese. She had taken to openly insulting and making fun of Jane in the last week or two as a way to try and gauge Nicholas's responses. He always seemed to have the correct reactions, he laughed and nodded in agreement, but her paranoia was increasing anyway.

Nicholas had landed the part of Romeo two days before. Everyone assumed he would and that made Alison feel proud but even more nervous about her potential failure. She knew the part of Juliet was between her, Jane sodding Pritchard and a third actor called Hayley Gibson, who was good but probably not quite good enough. Alison hoped if she couldn't impress the teachers, then perhaps Hayley would bring something she hadn't shown in any previous lesson, anything to stop the clamorous Jane from joining the Capulet crew.

Nicholas was attending the audition in his role of Romeo, reading lines opposite the leading lady hopefuls. The classic balcony scene had been chosen.

'Alphabetical order, ladies,' a voice – Miss Mullins, the head drama teacher – commanded from the middle of the rehearsal room. 'Hayley, you're first.'

There was a foldaway ladder for the women to climb – a balcony of sorts.

Alison thought about the height of the ladder and the depth of Romeo and Juliet's thwarted love; the distance from the balcony to the ground; the distance between them because of the familial feud.

Alison watched Hayley rush up the steps. She certainly seemed happy to perform first. She smiled at Nicholas, who gave her a nod and a thumbs-up. He was kind to everyone.

'Ready?' Miss Mullins asked.

The young actors nodded to her.

'Continue, please.'

'… and sails upon the bosom of the air,' Nicholas said, finishing his dialogue.

'O Romeo, Romeo! Wherefore art thou, Romeo?' Hayley projected the dialogue, looking beneath her feet as if she might have trodden on her star-crossed lover by accident.

'Thank you, that will be fine for today, Hayley, very nice,' Miss Mullins said. Alison had the scene memorised and was surprised the actors had been stopped in their tracks. She guessed Miss Mullins wasn't very impressed. She always made it very clear during lessons when she was struggling to tell a particular actor they weren't hitting the right notes, as she called them, as if they were musicians. Alison often wanted to question what the right notes actually were, and perhaps the teacher could demonstrate them, but that would probably be career suicide. Mullins carried a huge amount of influence both in the drama school and with agents and theatres outside.

'Alison, you're on next. Are you prepared?'

Was she prepared? That seemed an odd question to ask, and she hadn't asked Hayley the same thing, or anything similar. Did Alison look less than prepared, or have that reputation? Her head was full of cold by now, the paracetamol had worn off and she hadn't taken any ibuprofen. She felt hot, her body ached and her anxiety levels were on the rise.

Nicholas smiled at her with complete encouragement and faith, and that produced a moment of confidence in her, a moment that washed away all the illness and stress funk from inside her. She already was his Juliet and the audition would only confirm that. They had real chemistry. All she needed to do was say the lines with emotional conviction and remember the infernal theories. Be Juliet. You are Juliet.

Alison didn't enjoy heights. She never used the word vertigo when describing her fear to friends and family, but the amplification of listlessness and an unsteady sense of re-learning balance that came from her head feeling full of cotton wool made the top of the ladder feel a long, long way from the floor, as if she couldn't stand up there and say anything other than, 'I want to get down. I want to go home. I don't feel well.'

'Ready?' came the inevitable question.

'Yep,' Alison said. She smiled down at Nicholas, who, though he smiled back, could clearly see the slow wilt of his girlfriend.

Alison glanced at Jane Pritchard, who was smiling, reading a text of the play.

Fuck you, Prickhard, Alison thought. She breathed in and out and began.

'… and I'll no longer be a Capulet,' Alison said. She touched her forehead with emotion, her skin felt cold and clammy.

Nicholas looked up and moved forward. 'Shall I hear more?'

'Thank you both. That's great. Just enough,' Miss Mullins said, interrupting again, truncating the performance. 'Thank you, Alison, very nice.' Perhaps that was how these things worked, whether the right notes were being hit or not.

Nicholas gave Alison a hug and whispered, 'Well done' in her ear. She forced a smile but assumed she had blown the part. Jane bitchy bitch Prickhard was next up. The last performer, if they were any good, was always the one who was remembered, not the hack in the middle, Alison thought, as she sat down. She took some ibuprofen and a bottle of water from her handbag and waited for the last audition to begin. What had Miss Mullins meant by Just enough?

Halfway through the audition, Alison could see by the look on Miss Mullins' face – a combination of happy accident and reassurance – that her presumptions about Jane were right, that Jane Pritchard was always going to be Juliet Capulet. Alison watched Nicholas for any signs of additional Montague swooning for Jane – she couldn't see any – and the two actors were allowed to go through to the end of the scene.

'You were really good up there,' Nicholas said, as

they walked back to his flat. 'How do you feel it went?'

Alison was feeling angry and ill, and without any reason wanted to turn on her lover, berate him for allowing Jane the opportunity to shine, that he could, and should, have found a way to scupper her chances.

'I think we both know Jane got the job,' she said, blowing her nose and sniffing loudly after.

'Not for sure. I thought Hayley was a bit forced, but you were so good. I felt with you as if the words we were saying were our own, and—'

'Please, Nick, can we leave this now, please? I feel bloody ill and tired, and I wasn't really good up there. I was mediocre. Jane was really good and, as much as I despise her, she's your Juliet.'

Alison knew he was hurt, but he took her hand anyway and they walked home.

Two days later, Alison told Nicholas she hadn't got the part and he hugged her and said it was a stupid mistake, and that Jane Pritchard would make end up making a fool of herself. Alison had been offered the part of The Nurse, Juliet's servant, and she had taken it, regardless of the humiliation of playing second fiddle to her nemesis. She had to remain close to Nicholas throughout the play, and if ignominy was the only way, so be it.

Perhaps, she thought, I will become like Miss Peters and Jane Pritchard will be the next Marianne Jean-Baptiste, but Nicholas is more important than any Oscar nomination.

Rehearsals began the following week, and as they progressed, Alison began to notice subtle, incremental changes in her boyfriend's behaviour: his body language; his concentration towards Jane, both during scenes and in conversations after.

She knew she would have to fight to keep her Romeo.

Ben

Ben Goodson had grown up feeling as if he had the makings of a great artist inside him. He had ideas constantly about shape, words and colour, and ways to convert what he saw into other ways of seeing them from the earliest point in his life he could remember. The only problem he attached to the feelings was which art form would consume his time and effort? He won school writing competitions, suffering the embarrassment of having one of his teenage poems read by the headmaster during an assembly: 'I think we can all agree that was a fantastic effort. Well done, Ben. A round of applause, please everyone,' the Headmaster said. Ben wanted to force-feed the manuscript to the Head.

He suffered at the hands of sarcastic friends for days after the assembly. They thought it was hilarious to keep beginning sentences to him, 'Roses are red, violets are blue…'

He passed A-Level art with a series of painted portraits. He was told how wonderful they were by his classmates, but they felt like doodles that took longer than usual, as if he had done the bare minimum to impress his teachers and the examiners.

His form teacher asked him, 'Which artists influenced your work, Ben?' He said Lucian Freud and Frank Auerbach, not necessarily because it was true, more because he didn't want to have to try and explain why he did what he did. The painting just was to him. Did Freud or Auerbach have to answer for the influence in their work?

The main artistic issue he found after leaving university – he had taken an English degree, which had bored him with constant analytical theory – was that he lacked specific focus.

He felt as if art and literature came too easy to him. He wasn't arrogant about that fact, far from it. He didn't talk about his work to his friends or family, with the exception of David, who he met at uni and was a talented painter too. He just felt a deep sense of ennui about where he should try and end up with his talents. Serious application could mean a lifetime of productivity and happiness, but to apply time and energy to a lesser talent could be his ruin. He often thought of the Henry Wallis painting of Thomas Chatterton, pale and poisoned on his bed with the torn remains of his poetry littered in a grief-stricken heap by his limp, dead hand.

Then he read Nausea and it changed his life but not because of Sartre's words, although some passages made a lot of sense to him: "My thought is me: that's why I can't stop. I exist because I think…and I can't stop myself from thinking. At this very moment – it's frightful – if I exist, it is because I am horrified at existing."

It wasn't the existential angst of the words that lit an emotional fire within him; it was the cover design of the novel: the black and white photograph. There was a chiaroscuro sense of fear and anxiety in the image: a man looking up and over something; his eyes locked as if he can see his end, or the end of someone close to him, clearly. Ben studied every inch of the photograph, making pencil sketch reproductions of certain details: the reflective qualities in the man's eyes; the slight uplift of a sneer or smile or recognition of undiluted panic in his mouth. He knew he had to try and create the same feeling in photographs for other people. That could be his connection to art. He might just have discovered the perfect symbiosis for his talents: the malleable quality of the living form captured on film; the endless possibilities of exposure after exposure. He had to buy a camera and begin.

He took some months putting together a portfolio, sending work out to various galleries, all to no avail. There were lots of encouraging responses but no offers of exhibitions or jobs. Ben considered applying to an art school. It might be a chance to refine his work and make contacts. He had filled in two application forms, including one to Goldsmiths where David was studying fine art – they were sharing a flat in London too – when he received a letter offering him an interview as a photographer's assistant.

'So, Ben, this is good work. It's raw and your techniques are a bit immature, but what I really like about it is the choice of subjects and the composition. Any questions?' said Michael Garland, the fashion photographer who had contacted him.

'How did you find out about me?' Ben asked.

'Ah, the art world seeks out talent all the time. People talk at gallery openings and parties, usually about bollocks, but they pass on names too. Alice McKay at the Panoramic told me about you.'

Ben nodded and smiled. He remembered meeting Alice McKay. She had been completely offhand. She avoided eye contact with him, skimmed through his portfolio as if the images made her nauseous, and treated him as if he was the last person in the world she had any time for. He assumed she thought him a dilettante.

'So, how would you like to join my studio? It won't be glamorous, but you will learn how to shoot.'

Ben wasn't instantly gripped by the idea of fashion photography. He wasn't interested in clothes or supermodels. Was it even art?

Surely the work would be about Champagne smiles and air-kisses and saying things like, 'You look amazing, darling. Now smile like you've just had sex!'

He knew it was an in – a leg-up. He said, 'Yes please.'

The first few months were no more than lifting and carrying work. He often imagined himself carrying a hod of bricks up a ladder. He made tea for Michael, handed him different cameras and lenses, and hated the word tripod more than any other in the English language.

Ben also had the job of meeting and greeting the

models, pouring the damn Champagne and lighting seemingly endless Marlboro Lights. Most of the models treated him like a doorman with an emerging case of leprosy, but there was one exception, a regular visitor to the studio, a very beautiful French model called Stephanie Jaboudon.

'Bonjour, Benny,' she said. She had asked his name the first time they met. She was the first person he had ever allowed to call him Benny, and the last.

Ben didn't know or care about Michael Garland's sexuality. He never seemed interested sexually in the models, male or female, and was all about the work. So Ben made sure he also kept a completely professional approach at all times before, during and after a shoot. But he found his mind wandering every time Stephanie was in front of the camera. He watched her smile. The lighting made her red lips sparkle. She turned her head this way and that on Michael's instructions, and threw her head back laughing. Each change of clothing created the idea of a life being lived out in front of his eyes. She could be his muse, his one creative vision, like Lee Miller and Man Ray so many years before. She could be his future.

He didn't care about intelligent design or evolution. He just knew she was perfection.

'I was wondering how long you're in London for this time?' Ben said, as he helped Stephanie put her coat on. Her car was waiting outside.

'Why? Do you want to take me out, Benny?' she said, smiling.

Ben tried to suppress any signs of boyish

blurt-laughter or flushing of his cheeks.

'Yes I would,' he said, slowly and quietly. 'I would like to take you out.'

'Okay. Let's have breakfast at Patisserie Valerie on Old Compton Street tomorrow morning. Nine o'clock. Okay with you?'

'Perfect. I'll see you there.'

The breakfast was short and full of lust-filled stares. They were soon back at Stephanie's hotel, in her bed, with Ben trying to silence the voice in his head that kept repeating the same sentence: 'She's too good for you.'

'I have to fly to Paris later. It's my father's birthday on Friday. Would you like to come?' Stephanie shouted from the bathroom.

Ben sat up in bed, looked out of the large window to his right at St Paul's Cathedral in the middle distance and wanted to shout, 'Yes! Paris! Yes!' But he had two more shoots between then and Friday evening. Should he choose a job or a flight of love to Paradise?

'I can't this time, I'm sorry. I have to work. Michael would fire me,' he said, putting on a robe and walking to the bathroom doorway.

Stephanie was applying some eyeliner. She stopped and made a sad-clown expression into the mirror back at him.

'I know, I know. C'est merde, eh?' he said.

'Oui,' she replied, then turned and kissed him. 'Will you at least come with me to Heathrow?'

'Of course. When's your flight?'

She looked at her watch.

'About three hours from now. I need to pack and

leave.'

'I'll shower and get ready,' he said.

Stephanie pinched his backside as he walked away and he caught sight of her winking at him in the bathroom mirror. He wanted to stop, turn around and ask her to stay with him, or perhaps tell her he would go to Paris. Who needed the lifting and carrying of tripods anyway? He could meet her father and the rest of her family, stay in France, set up his own studio and begin his real career with her. But he kept walking and soon felt the warm spray of the shower muddle his thinking. By the time he was dry, Stephanie was ready to leave and he had to dress quickly. They held hands in the car on the way to the airport, hardly talking, and kissed long and deep before she passed through into the departure area.

'When will you be back?' he said.

'A few weeks. I'll text you soon. Au revoir,' she said, giving him one last kiss.

He walked to the Tube station; the car service had left after they were dropped off. He wondered if he had missed the chance of his life, followed conventional reason when he expected himself to do the opposite. Had her offer to join her family in a very personal way – a birthday – been her litmus test of his intentions and interest? Had he failed the test and ultimately lost the most vivid and sublime expression of his ideals so far?

He sat in the virtually empty Tube train and re-alised, smiling grimly and shaking his head, that he wouldn't even have the chance to say the hackneyed line: 'We'll always have Paris.'

David

White chocolate and blue-label *Smirnoff*?

David looked at the rest of the contents of the fridge-freezer. It all seemed familiar: organic beef mince, a frozen chicken, oven chips and leftovers in plastic storage boxes. The unusual confectionary and vodka stood out like deep-hidden secrets, finally revealed in all their contempt for the way things were supposed to be, like the ripples that begin a tsunami. He had no idea Sarah liked vodka, especially the hard stuff, or white chocolate. As he closed the fridge-freezer, holding the chocolate bar and the Smirnoff, he wondered what else had he never found out about the love of his life so far?

He poured himself a generous glass, snapped off three lines – four squares in each – of the white and very sweet tasting fun food and put the rest of the bottle and chocolate bar back where they were as best he could remember. Fun food was Sarah's term for junk food. It was how she referred to burgers, chocolates and cakes. She had a habit of making him feel bad on Saturday trips to the supermarket when ever he placed a packet of Jaffa Cakes or the occasional special offer double-pack of the supermarket's own brand milk chocolate into the deepest recess of the trolley. He knew he was pathetic to behave in such a childish and covert fashion. He could have just said aloud that he fancied something sweet, but he usually made a 'Caught me red-handed!' face and put the fun food back on the relevant shelf.

David took his drink and chocolate and sat on his armchair opposite the television sighing at the familiarity of the cushions. The room smelled of polish and the floors looked vacuumed. He guessed Sarah had cleaned the place as soon as he left the last time. The sense of his home made his stomach drop. He realised, looking at the framed reproduction Modigliani that they had bought only a month before, he was here but not really here. Not in the physical or metaphysical sense, but insofar that he wasn't supposed to be in the house at that moment. He had finally given his house keys back to Sarah but had a spare set cut, telling himself it was as much about an emergency as anything underhand. Sarah, who had travelled back to Kent to stay with her parents, assumed he was staying with Alison. Alison thought he was staying the night at Ben and Richard's flat to work on the short film.

I could just disappear tonight, he thought, just wander into the sea somewhere and drift away for ever. Or I could spend the night and tomorrow building a refuge for myself in the loft, tie a rope ladder to the roof beams, soundproof the flooring and still live here. He stared into space and then at the sofa which

Sarah had made her own when they watched television or a film, or when she read books or a newspaper. He sometimes watched her as she read and wanted to talk to her about the way he felt he was going wrong in his life, the mistakes he had made. They had bought a house too young and made too many financial commitments too soon. He wanted to paint and travel to many places with her, to experience many different versions of life, not just begin surburban domesticity in their mid-twenties. But he never told her. Instead he fell in love with someone else. He never gave Sarah the chance to laugh at his Bohemian ideals or explain why they had made a good decision investing in property and they could still travel every year, painting and experiencing other cultures. He became more and more anxious. He had signed his life away without really thinking things through. Sarah suffered for his insecurities. What was to stop him becoming just as much of a soft, domestic, full-of-hot-air man with Alison?

He drank the last of his vodka and walked back to the kitchen, poured himself another glass and decided he would top up the bottle with water before he left.

He sat at the dining room table and looked at the depleted bookshelves. His novels were in boxes at Alison's flat. Various Margaret Atwood novels caught his eye, lying on top of each other, and the box set of Anthony Powell's A Dance to the Music of Time series stood out in all its pristine condition, which Sarah had never opened or read. He expected her to hand it back to him any time soon. Or perhaps she would put it in the recycling bin with the wedding file. And then maybe the pulped paper would find its way into the bloody products he had to pretend to enjoy marketing. Wouldn't that be joyfully ironic?

'What am I doing here?' he said to his reflection in the window behind his chair. The front bay window curtains were drawn and Sarah used a timer-switch to keep some lights on in the evening, so he didn't think anyone would be suspicious about his presence in the house. Had Sarah even told the neighbours about their break-up yet? Had she warned them that he was a sneaky, lying bastard who might try to find his way back in? Were the police outside already, waiting to take him into custody as soon as he opened the front door clutching the Anthony Powell books and the last of the white chocolate?

David laughed at himself and swigged down the majority of the glass of vodka, smacking his lips wide as the cold liquid made a tickling burn in his throat. He was beginning to feel drunk.

He knew exactly why he had come back. He wanted one last night alone in the house; one last opportunity to find things to take away with him; things that might seem bizarre to any other person but which he would carry with him for ever; his own memento mori collection of what might seem like ephemera, to represent the life he had left behind – the life he had killed.

As he poured yet another full glass of vodka he knew he would have to replace the bottle the following day. He took a long sip, standing with his back against the dishwasher. He noticed the spotless hob top, the gleam of the kitchen sink and the way everything in the kitchen had never looked as well ordered before. Then he glanced at the cupboard door with the wonky hinge. He leaned down and opened and closed it. Someone had repaired it. Sarah? Had she been perfectly able to fix the hinge all the time but waited for him to get his act together and prove himself? They had always shared the basic DIY bits and pieces in the house: new lightbulbs, changing plugs etc. It made sense that she might have decided, in the act of cleansing the house post-him, to take on the outstanding tasks that his efforts had fallen well short of providing any kind of resolution for.

David lurched to the right dramatically, aware of his increasing levels of drunkenness, as he walked from the dining room into the lounge, and felt a moment of embarrassment as if Sarah was right there shaking her head in dismay. He smiled into the mirror over the fireplace where he had stood to make his departure announcement a few days before – it already felt like weeks – and contorted his features to make them repugnant: puffed out cheeks and wide eyes; his tongue pushing his bottom lip out as he squinted and forced his chin to double.

Then the telephone rang.

He dropped his glass in shock, looked around the room, to the dining table, and into the kitchen. The phone rang three times. He almost answered it until the ansaphone clicked into action.

'I'm not here at the moment, please leave a message,' Sarah's voice said.

Already ditched my message, he thought, not wanting to speak, irrationally believing he might be heard by the caller.

'Hi, Sarah, it's me, Ben. I just wanted to call you to say that's fine about the text. I'd be happy to talk. And as far as helping Dave clear out, that's cool too. I guess it must be really hard for you at the moment. I'll text you to let you know I called…that's a bit ridiculous though, isn't it, calling and texting? Okay, anyway, speak to you soon. Bye.'

The elongated beep of the machine let David breathe out. He looked at the map-like vodka stain on the carpet, closed his eyes and swore, and then went to the kitchen to get a soapy sponge.

'She'll know I've been here now,' he said. 'God damn it.'

As he scrubbed, his mind swung like a pendulum, picking up speed, between anxiety about his plan to come and go in the house without anyone ever knowing and how he had foiled himself by being such a scaredy cat when the phone rang; then to thoughts about his presence in his own house and why there was no good or legal reason for him not to be anywhere in his own property at any time he pleased, as long as he respected her space and her things – like the vodka and the white chocolate.

He would buy more of the white chocolate too.

What about Ben? Why had he called? What text? Had Sarah been contacting all his friends, trying to organise some kind of post-split intervention where all the people David cared about told him what a fool he was and how badly he treated people? How could he bring up the ansaphone message when he spoke to Ben without compromising his best friend? He wanted to replay the message, but there was absolutely no way of doing that without blowing the whole secrecy ruse.

'Ignore the sodding call. Ben was just being nice, trying to placate Sarah. She wants me out asap. I get it,' David said to himself.

The sponge had dried and its ragged edges were coming away in bits with his persistent rubbing of the carpet. It was serving no purpose other than keeping his mind unfocused, his eyes staring through the simple movement of his hand.

David stood up and looked down at the stain. He had increased the damp width with his drunken efforts and thought he might get Sarah's hairdryer out in the morning to finish the job properly. Perhaps with a fresh bottle of vodka in the freezer and renewed levels of chocolate, plus a dry, stainless carpet, Sarah might never know he had been there. He stuffed the sponge into his pocket and replaced it with a new one from their cleaning cupboard, making sure it was the same design and colour.

'Well, I suppose, as I am going to buy new stock in the morning, I better finish off that booze and choccie,' he said. He opened the fridge and freezer doors, took the bottle out first and emptied the last of the vodka into his glass. He then put the fun food into his trouser pocket, feeling the sponge under his fingers. The connection of things in and from the house reminded him why he had come in the first place.

What should he take? What could Sarah do without and never even notice had been taken away?

'She won't miss that sponge…or the vodka bottle and chocolate wrapper,' he said, looking around the kitchen. There was an empty brown leather key fob by the toaster with the emblem of the city of Edinburgh printed onto a silver disc in the centre. David bought it for Sarah when they visited the annual arts festival three years before. She had kept her keys on it ever since, and now it had been discarded like the ansaphone greeting.

'Fine. I'll have that back. I did buy it. And I need a new one,' he muttered. He could hear consternation growing in his voice and tried to calm down. Remember, you left her, he thought, putting the spare house key on the fob and then stuffing it into his jacket pocket.

He reached up to the top of the glass and mug cupboard and brought down the backdoor keys and went into the back garden, clutching his vodka and snapping off chocolate from his trouser pocket. He stood for a few seconds, enjoying the mixture of sweetness and warmth in his mouth and throat with his eyes closed, breathing in the spring scents, and then he looked towards the neighbours' walls to gauge any interest in him. There didn't seem to be anyone around. He walked a few paces and sat on the dividing wall between the unfinished patio and the whirly dryer. He couldn't resist flicking the low-hanging wires, which had always made putting out the washing a game of 'How much weight to apply on each of the three sides without the whole thing collapsing...'

David guessed Sarah might use the tumble dryer until her father finishing the concrete embedding job. He tried to straighten the whirly dryer – one final nod to domestic success in his time. It stood erect for a few minutes and then drooped again. He wanted to take a hammer to it but settled for a kick to the base, which made his toes ache.

'Why am I out here? Come on, Dave, get it together,' he said quietly. He was there for a reason and couldn't allow his emotions to dictate every movement.

He leaned down and pulled a few handfuls of grass and earth up, pushed them into his jacket pockets and then dragged off clumps of sage from the bush Sarah had cultivated next to the back door. He went back inside after that and re-locked the door, taking a last glance up the patchy lawn to the back wall.

'Okay,' he whispered as if a prepared plan was on time and his efficiency had reached its zenith.

David started to walk towards the stairs and noticed the photographs missing from the wall next to the bookshelves. He didn't have any memory of what the images had been, except one black and white Ben had taken of the two of them, but he guessed he had been in all the missing shots.

He looked in on the progress of the vodka stain.

The mark was less pronounced but still very obviously the site of a spill.

'Hairdryer in the morning for you, matey,' he said to the carpet.

The flash of the ansaphone messages received reminded him of the world outside, and that not long from now Ben might be sitting in his armchair, talking to Sarah with her legs tucked under her backside – the concentrated way she sat when she wanted to talk something through to the end – both of them holding cups of tea. Ben would listen well and nod sympathetically, saying the right things, and the best part was that David hadn't involved his friend in the growth of the relationship with Alison at any stage. Of course they had met during the making of the film and twice after for re-shoots, but Ben's hands were clean of any duplicity.

It was only right that Sarah should have some way of separating herself from David through his friends. Ben would act the way methadone was supposed to for heroin addicts: a gradual withdrawal. Eventually, Sarah wouldn't hear from Ben anymore. He would slip away, as friends do when they are silently obliged to make a choice between partners who have split up. Ben was his friend. And he remained loyal.

David nodded in satisfaction that he was emotionally backed up. He had a wingman and so did Sarah.

He slurped down the very last drops of the vodka, put the glass on the dining room table, wiped his mouth with the back of his hand and began to climb the stairs, holding on to the rail tightly. His legs felt tingly and loose. He reached the top and made sure he didn't let go of the banister until he was some way from the edge of the last stair. As he walked towards their bedroom – Sarah's bedroom – he looked up at the loft hatch and whispered, 'I may be seeing you soon, darkness, my old friend.'

The bedroom had been changed. Sarah had moved the wardrobe, the bed, and the chest of drawers with dressing table and its top-mounted three-way mirror.

She had replaced posters and photographs. It all looked so different that David had to stop in the centre of the room and remember how it had been only a few days ago. He noticed dust on the carpet and linen basket, and thought some part of him might remain in the house for ever, his dead skin woven into the fibres of the building, regardless of scrubbing, painting and hours of vacuuming.

'Jesus, has it come to that? That I want to be remembered as dead skin?' he asked himself.

He sat at Sarah's dressing table and looked into each of the three mirrors. His cheeks were florid and the area around his eyes looked dark.

He sprayed some of Sarah's Chanel perfume on to his wrists, rubbed them together and breathed in deeply. The poignancy of the smell and its references in his memory almost made him cry.

He opened the strawberry flavoured lip salve that Sarah constantly applied during the winter months and began slathering it on to his lips in circles until the greasy texture made his mouth feel heavy. Then he put the lip salve in his jacket pocket.

There was a clean and ironed blouse – a work blouse – hanging on the outside of one of the wardrobe doors. David took it off the door and pressed his face into the material. Another memory appeared, clear this time.

'Do you really like it? I was thinking of taking it back. I kept the receipt,' Sarah had said, the previous year, when she bought the blouse.

'It looks great. You look great. I love the way it shows off your waist and breasts,' he had replied. She had laughed and rolled her eyes. He meant to say that she looked beautiful. He should have told her that then and a lot more often.

He guessed the blouse might be given away. Or that some other man would some day soon say how much he liked the way it showed off her beauty. And that other guy would probably use the right words.

David whirled around the bedroom in a spinning dance with the blouse.

'The very thought of you, the sheer idea of you…' he sang. He was remembering the Ella Fitzgerald album Sarah had bought him as a Valentine's Day present the previous year. The song was their favourite and they had danced together as it played after supper on that special day. Sarah always thought Valentine's Day corny and commercial, but she made sure she bought him something nice each year anyway, and he did the same for her.

He hadn't been through any birthdays, Christmases or Valentines with Alison yet. He wondered how different things would be, beginning again, eliciting details about special desires or presents, or the type of greeting card Alison might prefer: something 'occasion specific' or something arty and tasteful? He guessed arty; she was an actor. The lack of knowledge and the doubt in his mind about what Alison might or might not like made him feel suddenly vulnerable and sad. Who was she? David replaced the blouse on the wardrobe door, stroking it one last time.

He sat on the double bed and lay back.

The room was so quiet. He could hear a slight wheeze in his breathing. He reached into his jacket pocket, pushing the collected items to one side, and took out his Salbutamol inhaler. Two puffs, then a third. He held his breath until he started to feel lightheaded then breathed out.

He moved back up the bed and put his head on Sarah's pillow. Then he sat up suddenly. An idea, a possibility, had occurred to him. He turned around and looked down at the pillow-case. There were a few strands of Sarah's light brown hair lying on a corner. He lifted them up, wound them into a small circle, put them on his tongue and swallowed them.

'Now I can keep your DNA with mine,' he said, feeling an irritation in his throat, swallowing harder to force the hair down.

It was stuffy in the room, so he opened all the windows. A breeze immediately lifted the net curtains up in time with each other. They looked to David as if they were trying to wave him away: 'Get out of this room, you invader. You are no longer wanted or needed.'

He put his head back on Sarah's pillow, pushed his nose into the pillowcase and sniffed it, up and down, side to side, over and over again. The smell of her skincare products – so familiar in their scent, yet he couldn't have named the branding if his life had depended on it – made him cry. He wanted to come home and stay.

'I've fucked it all up,' he said.

He felt pathetic and annoyed with himself very soon after the crying began. The din of self-pity sobered him slightly and he knew he had to make clear-headed decisions in the morning and thereafter. Not on that bed. Something had torn him away from Sarah in the first place and he needed time to think when his head was clear. He could, and would, talk it through with Ben.

He watched the blouse on the wardrobe door lift and fall with the breeze. The arms went this way and that. The coat hanger swung gently. He smiled and closed his eyes.

'The very thought of you…' he sang again, very quietly this time.

Sarah

Sarah wrote and re-wrote her first post-split text to Ben several times. First on paper. Her scribbling out of words which she thought might be perceived as misleading in the future began to depress her. There was something to be said for the same font size of emails and texts (no emotional calligraphy involved, just words) and the clean look of digital messages – clean but sometimes sterile. Reconnecting post split with a mutual friend, she was aiming to combine warm and engaging with a pragmatic and dry-eyed look to the future. She wanted Ben to read the message, then perhaps have to re-read it a couple of times, looking for a hidden meaning or two. She wanted him intrigued by her.

After numerous drafts she picked up her mobile phone and began. She held the phone in her left hand and keyed the letters carefully with her right index finger, steering well clear of the send key. She had recently bought her first touchscreen phone and found the level of acute sensitivity on the keypad incredibly frustrating. She had sent a few misspelled texts and work emails already, and as someone working in town council marketing and PR, it was essential to create the right impression of understanding facts and various scenarios, boiling down potentially damaging policies or local 'issues' for the Press. She checked and re-checked her phrasing, her grammar and finally her punctuation – as if a misplaced comma could be the making or breaking of the rest of her life. After one final read-through, she pressed send and watched the conversation bubble icon drift across the screen to acknowledge the message had gone.

She had the weekend ahead, plenty of thinking time, and she was back in her childhood bedroom. She lay down on her bed and felt relieved to be somewhere comforting and familiar, surrounded by people who loved her. Her sister was coming for lunch the following day. But there was a nagging in her conscience that she had run away from something important, some kind of whisper in her life that had begun when David told her he was leaving. Was it about Ben? Or was some part of her subconscious still in love with David and fighting to be heard against her conscious mind, which had taken to full-throated denial. She had cried a lot. She had been without sleep. And she had hated watching David pack and go. But then she had taken a metaphorical deep breath, cleaned the house as if it was up for sale, bought some of her favourite things – there was a bar of white chocolate and a bottle of blue-label Smirnoff awaiting her return – and finally sat down in what was now her home, her house. She had begun to think about things. Think about people. About Ben.

Why the hell shouldn't she? David was doubtless shagging that Alison bitch every night and day, so why shouldn't she begin to think of her own needs?

The Ben situation was so complicated. They had shared one very intimate dance: one moment on one evening. They hadn't kissed or slept together and Ben had never given her any hint of strong feelings he might have for her. Maybe he danced like that with everyone. He and David had been crazy-drunk one night in the past and danced a bad tango with each other. Did that mean Ben was in love with him too?

She closed her eyes and tried to remember the dance: Ben's eyes locked on hers; the music; her hands shaking, wanting to stroke his face.

Her parents had given her all the usual reassurances that she would get over David – give it time – and they were always there for her – anything you need. Her father had driven her up from the railway station after she arrived. He hadn't said much in the car, turning and smiling at her occasionally, probably thinking to himself how much he wanted to punch, and keep punching, David's face. He had never liked David, thought him self-interested and too cocky about everything, a fake authority on any given subject. When ever she had talked about real things, like finishing the patio or a loft conversion, David's eyes had glazed over. She knew her father wanted to confront David and demand to know what he wanted in his life.

'I've made your favourite meal,' her mum said, 'that Nigella Lawson stew.'

Sarah was being pampered. Her mum was trying to make her feel completely loved. She did feel cared for and happy to be away from her home for a couple of days. At the very least there was no chance of any visits from David.

'I'm going out for a walk, Mum,' Sarah called through the lounge door. 'Emma invited me over for a cup of tea and to meet her new baby.'

'Do you want me to drive you over?' her father offered, opening the door.

'No, but thanks.'

Sarah kissed her father on the cheek. There was a smell of beer on his breath and a hint of cigarette smoke. He was smiling, but his eyes betrayed parental stress.

'All right, love. See you later,' he said. He opened the front door and waved her goodbye.

Emma Richards was Sarah's oldest friend. They had met at primary school, lived around the corner from each other for years, and still spoke on the phone, texted or emailed each other every month. Emma had recently given birth to her first child, a boy called Sam, and Sarah had been planning a trip home to meet her godson.

As she walked up to Emma's front door, Sarah remembered the look of worry on David's face when she told him about Sam being born, as if that was a starting pistol for their own imminent entry into parenthood. She thought it was funny at the time, but it made her angry now to think about his motives and reasons, his lies, in so many things they had discussed as part of a future life together.

'Hey!' Emma shouted as she opened the door. She flung her arms around Sarah's neck and hugged her long and hard.

Emma's husband, Adrian, came out of the kitchen holding Sam over his shoulder. He smiled at Sarah, kissed her on the cheek and turned the baby around to show him off.

'Looks like Yoda from Star Wars, eh?' Adrian said. 'Smaller ears perhaps.'

Sarah looked at the scrunched-up face, the closed eyes, the puckered mouth and the hands that looked too small to hold even a single grape. Her eyes began to fill with tears.

'It's okay, it's all right. Would you like to hold him?' Emma said. She touched Sarah's shoulder and pressed gently.

'Yeah, that would be really nice. I've never held one before.'

Sarah dried her eyes with her sleeve, took the linen cloth Adrian had draped over his shoulder – 'In case he pukes on you,' he said – and then she received the baby. He was heavier than he looked, and floppy. She cupped his head quickly and held him close to her chest.

As she walked around the lounge making small talk to Sam and smiling at his parents, she remembered a conversation with David, a very recent conversation, reiterating their shared desire to have four children together. Together.

They had come up with names – Jack, Rose, Niamh and Theo – and talked at length about how they would divide the childcare. Sarah suggested she take at least six months' maternity leave, maybe eight, depending on how she was coping, and then perhaps David could take unpaid leave until the first of the four was old enough to attend nursery. They could repeat the pattern as the other children came along. 'One every other year or something,' David said.

He seemed so pleased with the ideas, with his suggestions about converting the spare bedrooms into 'areas of colour and light' for their 'mass progeny'.

As she stared into the back garden at the grass needing a cut, wet from recent rain, and the shed door swinging open and shut, Sarah wondered how deep David's lies and deceit ran.

Sam seemed to be getting heavier by the second. Sarah began to feel her arms aching. She wondered if there was etiquette to how long a person is supposed to hold a new baby before handing it back.

'Heavy little monkey, isn't he?' Adrian said, seeming to read her thoughts. Sarah had always liked Adrian. He had gone to the same secondary school as Emma and Sarah. 'Shall I relieve you?' he added, holding his hands out.

'Thanks. I'm so unfit. I feel like a weakling now.'

'The night time is the worst,' Emma said. 'I knew it would be, but man alive, he wants to be fed and fed. Then there's the walking him around, winding him and getting him back to sleep.

'Any chance of some tea, Ade?'

'Certainly, my lady. Would you hold him while I get the kettle on?'

Adrian brought two mugs of tea back, collected Sam and walked off to another room. Sarah wondered if he had been briefed before she arrived. She imagined Emma dishing out the orders: 'When we get to the tea, I want you to take Sam off for a bit, so we can talk.'

'How are you?' Emma asked. 'I suppose that's a completely dumb question considering your whole existence has been folded inside out. But how are you?' She squeezed Sarah's hand and sat back to listen.

'Pretty much all right actually. I know my tears of joy when I met Sam, who is beautiful by the way, betrayed a hint of melancholy, and I am reeling a bit from the sudden change of everything. But who wouldn't be?'

'Do you mind me asking you frank questions?' Emma said.

'Course not, Em.' Sarah sipped her tea and smiled. Emma was exactly the right person to open up to, the one person she could eventually express her feelings for Ben to.

'Do you know what made David…well, go after that other woman?'

Sarah wasn't expecting an opener like this. She thought the questions would be about her emotional state, her plans for the coming days, the house, and what she wanted to do with her life now.

'He's a guy. He wanted some fresh meat, I guess. I don't know, Em. You'd have to ask him.' Sarah could hear a tone of mild annoyance growing in her voice. 'Sorry to be snappy. The one part of this whole shitty mess I can't deal with yet is the thought of him kissing and cuddling her… shagging her, making their little love pad cosy. I met her once, did I tell you that?'

'No way. When?'

'When David shot that bloody stupid short film of his. The thing about the medical student who amputated someone's arm. Do you remember me emailing you?'

Emma took two sips of tea, looked quizzical, then raised her eyebrows and nodded in acknowledgment.

'Yeah, yeah. You said the actress was prettier than you

expected, and that she worked with David. That's who he's gone off with?'

'Yeah, her. And I said she was a conceited little cow who was after someone's boyfriend. I thought she liked Ben at the time. He's David's best friend. He worked on the film too.'

Sarah had a sudden leap in her stomach, a feeling of warm joy that, as big a bitch as Alison was, at least she hadn't stolen Ben away.

'So did you beat the shit out of this Alison cow?' Emma said. She smiled and they both laughed.

'Not yet. Fuck her. She'll get her comeuppance with David eventually.'

'Were there any signs when they were making the film that she was interested in David?'

'Not really. I mean they had silly work-related in-jokes, but that was it. They seemed to get on well, but I honestly thought she was into Ben.'

Sarah was using Ben's name more and more, and was enjoying saying it aloud. He was out there waiting, maybe, if she had read the dance right, for her to open the way for them to be together. A real together, not like David's version.

'Jesus, Sarah. I am so sorry. I mean, you seem to be coping really well, but I know you were expecting to get married to David. How do you feel about that?'

Sarah took a moment. Images of the wedding that never happened passed through her head on fast forward. David might have spent the minutes before the marriage vows like Hugh Grant before his wedding in Four Weddings and a Funeral, only with no comedy involved, pouring his heart out to Ben about his new-found adoration of Alison, saying he couldn't pretend to have feelings for Sarah any longer. Perhaps, by that time, Sarah herself would have reached a conclusion about Ben, or just a sense of what David wasn't telling her or feeling for her anymore. If they had gone through with the wedding, would David, doubtless drunk and feeling free to air his soul, have blurted out how he had married the wrong woman, that he wanted a divorce as soon as possible?

Sarah's face twisted for a second with recognition of the close shave she had experienced.

'I feel okay. Better than okay actually. I want to talk to you about something, Em. Well, someone really. Thing is, I've realised in a very short time that David did us both a favour in leaving. I know that sounds odd and as if I'm in complete denial about my true feelings. I'm certain a psychiatrist would analyse my next words and tell me I'm deflecting grief or something, but the thing is, I'm in love with another guy.'

Emma's eyes shot wide open, as if she had been woken in the night by unknown voices downstairs.

'What? Really? Who?' she said.

'Ben.'

'Ben? Ben, as in David's friend, best friend, Ben?'

'Yes, that Ben,' Sarah said. 'Best friend to David Ben. Was going to be David's best man Ben. Best guy I know in the world Ben. And the man I love Ben.' She tried to smile, but a sadness gripped her. She would never be able to find her way into a relationship with this Ben. His friendship with David, his loyalty to some Unspoken Code about going out with ex-boyfriends or girlfriends would always stop him dead.

'Have you spoken to him yet?' Emma asked. She moved closer to Sarah, lowering her voice as if Adrian might be listening to every word, transcribing the conversation to send to David later that day.

'I've texted him, did that earlier, but it was a general text.'

'What kind of general?'

'Kind of "I'd like to chat about things. Would you help David clear out the last of his stuff?" That kind of general.'

'Right. Okay. Bloody hell, Sarah. This is a big shift. Are you sure you're ready to take on a new relationship so soon, and with someone so close to your ex-nearly-husband? You're still dealing with David going.'

'Well, no, I'm not ready to put my heart on the line to be crushed again. No, not at all. But I can't stop thinking about Ben. It's not something that's just started recently. We had a dance. We shared a truly pure moment of… well, ecstasy, without drugs or too much alcohol. It was glorious. I looked at him and -'

'Hang on a second, Sarah.'

Emma stood up and went upstairs. Sarah heard her talking to Adrian. Then she came back down and took her place on the sofa.

'Sorry, I realised Sam's due for a feed soon, but he's asleep at the moment and Adrian's dozing too. So, tell me all the details of this dance, not just the last bit about your eyes meeting.'

'We – David, Ben and I – were out for a meal in town. Ben and I got into a silly argument about the meaning of a word - '

'Which word?'

'Beatific. But that really isn't too important. So we're arguing back and forth, and I'm thinking how stupid and male he's being, completely arrogant and, worst of all, completely wrong in what he's saying. But the other thing that hits me between the eyes is that I am so engrossed in Ben and his ridiculous assertions, I forget David is even with us until he tries to defuse everything by buying more drinks.

'It was so confusing. I didn't think I could suddenly become this woman who found another man so totally absorbing.'

'How were you absorbed by an argument?' Emma finished the last of her tea.

'Because I was feeling alive again. I don't mean that to sound all dramatic, and as if I've been in a loveless relationship with David for years and years. I mean that I was talking and thinking the way I did when I was younger, in university – perhaps the way David and I did once. Although now my memory is full of listening to David: his opinions, his dislikes and moans about politics and work and…well, it doesn't matter what else. The point is, I felt connected to Ben during that argument.'

'When did the dance thing happen?'

'Later that evening. We'd had a few more drinks and talked about not much of anything. I think Ben felt embarrassed or annoyed about the argument. I thought we would walk straight home and that would be it for the evening, same old, same old. But I saw a queue outside a club, and I knew they were having an indie music night. I just felt like I needed to dance and let off some steam. Of course David wanted to leave as soon as we got inside. His face was full of tension. He said he was tired and left.'

'Well that was a downer, wasn't it?' Emma said. She held her cup up as a silent offering of more tea. Sarah nodded and followed her to the kitchen.

'You'd think so, but I was just relieved. He can drain the fun out of anything. I feel like I've known that and put up with it for years, but now I don't have to. I felt a bit weird being in the club with just Ben, but as soon as he'd bought us drinks and we'd sat down, I started to feel as if something was meant to happen.'

'And what happened during the dancing?'

'We were both a bit inhibited at first, as you are, I suppose, when you're used to dancing with the same person for so many years. Not that David and I danced that much, usually at weddings when he was too drunk to think about what he was doing - '

'Sarah.'

'Yeah, what's up?'

'I'm sorry to stop you, but to be honest, you are my oldest friend…and to be completely honest, you do sound as if you're harbouring a lot of anger towards David. You keep punctuating what you're saying with derisive comments about him, and I'm wondering if this thing with Ben is a reaction to the grief of the split. I am aware you said people would make that exact assumption, but maybe there's some truth in it?'

Sarah took her second mug of tea, feeling annoyed, and walked back to the lounge. She glanced around at the squeaky, soft baby toys, the many family photographs, and the jumble of books and DVD cases. She thought about turning on Emma, asking her what gave her the right to tell Sarah how she felt. Emma had done Sociology at university and worked as a social worker for two years before Sam came along. Did that experience give her a special understanding; give her any real insight into the human condition?

Sarah sipped some tea and decided to keep calm. Giving in to any desire to shout and scream would merely cement the idea that she was on the rebound with her feelings for Ben and that she couldn't be trusted to make logical choices.

'Let me tell you about the dance first. I get what you're saying, Em, and I understand why you think it. I would too. But I need to tell you the rest.'

'Sure. I didn't mean to be a pain in the backside. I just want to be as honest as we've always been,' Emma said, stroking Sarah's arm. 'So you were dancing. Which song was playing?'

'What?'

'Which song was playing? Set the mood for me.'

'Siouxsie and the Banshees, Cities in Dust, I think.'

'Great song. Go on.'

'Well, I was frugging about, doing my usual swaying from side to side. Did I ever tell you that David called my - ah, okay, okay, keep away from the David comments, I know. Anyway, I was desperate to let go, just to dance as if nothing mattered, that's the point. I was watching Ben, who is a great dancer. He's got a fantastic body too, tall and lean, a bit like Ryan Gosling.'

'Jesus creepers, really? Like Ryan Gosling?'

'Very much like that. Same smile and eyes. Talking of eyes, it was when we locked onto each other, totally immersed...That sounds awful, doesn't it. Sorry. He looked at me and I looked at him. We got very close to each other without actually touching.'

'Then he kissed you?'

'No. We didn't touch before, during or after the dance. We just connected. I don't understand what really happened, but I felt it come together, and I'm certain he did too. That was before David said anything about the Alison bitch and before he said he was leaving. So you see, it isn't just a reaction to my split with David or a whim, or something equally as transitory.'

'Okay. All right. I am officially convinced. Ben is the one. I'm sorry for making that crappy pre-judgment in the kitchen. I should know better than that. Wow, this is big, Sarah. Did you ever have that kind of feeling with David?' Emma asked, putting the baby monitor to her ear.

'Everything okay up there?'

'Yeah, Adrian's snoring, bless him. He was up for hours with Sam last night.'

'Poor guy. And poor you. I guess it won't last.'

'Roll on six months. We can start sleep training then. So, did you ever feel that way with David?'

'Yes, I think so. But it's been a long time since I felt any explosion of emotional...joining in that way. It's so hard to explain. I loved David so much when we first started going out, and that lasted a long time: the passion; the sharing of ambition and goals; doing things together and really enjoying being a couple. But then something changed, maybe when we bought the house. Perhaps the level of domesticity and turning so much of our attention on the new home and away from us was the tipping point.'

'Has he tried to explain why he decided to leave you?'

Emma cupped her tea mug with both hands and glanced at the stairs. Sarah wondered if she was wearing out her welcome. Was she being completely selfish, consuming so much of her friend's much-needed energy?

'I haven't let him try. He's been in and out of the house all bloody week, collecting his rubbish from the loft. I know he's deliberately taking his time. He loves that house as much as I do. He probably wants me to leave instead.'

'I reckon, after a while, you should talk to him. Let him explain his reasons, as hard as that might be for you to hear. And then, if you're ready and you've spoken to Ben, perhaps you could tell David how you feel about him going and about your feelings for Ben too?'

'Why would I want to hear about David's desire for a new woman or tell him about how much he's hurt me? Why would I ever want to tell him about Ben?'

Emma looked at the up-and-down line of green dots on the baby monitor; the baby was crying.

'Because without being completely open and honest, you might miss out on something really special with Ben. You might regret not closing that chapter of your life with David.'

Alison

The closing night party for Romeo and Juliet was loud with self-congratulations. Cast members shouted their lines to each other, still wearing their costumes, and cheered each other with raised glasses of red wine. The drama teachers mingled with the lead characters. Nicholas and Jane stood next to each other and took occasional bows to thank the seemingly endless 'Bravo' and 'Fabulous' procession.

Alison was given a few verbal pats on the back, but the Nurse just wasn't an inspirational character; she was a facilitator, someone for Juliet to depend upon. Alison sipped her wine, staring at Nicholas grinning as if his face had become stuck in the same position. She doubted whether there would ever be a production of the play where the Nurse truly shone, unless some director-of-tomorrow decided to subvert the text. She had enjoyed being part of her first semi-professional stage piece: the concentration needed to learn her lines; keeping up with the other actors; feeling part of one of the most famous plays ever written; and she had Nicholas in her private moments, coaching her to find an emotional link to Juliet.

'The Nurse is the only person Juliet can trust. She is the sounding board, the rock, the mainstay for the intensity of Juliet's feelings. It's an incredibly important part, regardless of the so-called billboard roles in the play. Forget Jane as Jane, and see her only as Juliet. Okay?' Nicholas said. Alison knew he worked almost as hard on her part as his own. She felt a flicker of guilt growing each time he helped her. He was the leading man. He had an incredibly hard job to do. Regardless of his pedigree and abilities, he was still a student too.

A large part of Alison didn't care about the empathy of the Nurse, the connection to Juliet or the outcome of the play. The students had been told by Miss Mullins that theatrical agents always attended productions such as these. She just wanted Jane Pritchard to fail dismally and to keep her hands off Nicholas.

There was no good way to convey those feelings to Nicholas; no good time before the play. Perhaps when the thing was over and done she would have a chance to sit and explain to him about the depth of her love, about how much she depended on him, that he was the centre of her world. Would that sound silly and overly dramatic? Would he just put such an out-pouring down to actor-tendencies: the need to express oneself in undiluted ways both on and off the stage?

Alison tried to get close to Nicholas, wending her way through packs of students, who stood with arms around each other singing songs she didn't recognise or like, firing a volley of mixed Shakespearean quotes.

Jane Pritchard imperiously watched her approach. Her smile, so pure and true and radiant before, dropped into fakery.

A stagey smile, Alison thought. Smile as much as you like. Smile for Miss Mullins and the agents, smile for the next part and smile for anyone else in the fucking room, but now it's time to move away from my boyfriend, Bitchard.

'Fantastic work, Jane. You were so very good. That death scene always makes me want to cry, especially when you die. And tonight was the best death I could have imagined you ever having,' Alison said, close to Jane's face. She knew she was drunk and being deliberately rude, and she liked the feeling. Nicholas wasn't listening to them at that moment. He was talking to a man in a dark linen suit, who kept smiling and nodding and laughing. Alison wondered if he was an agent or a family member she might be introduced to later.

'Well, thanks, Alison, thanks a lot. That means a lot coming from you. It's a great role. You were really good too. You learned those lines like a pro. I was wondering if anyone would forget them. I hope you get to play a part like Juliet one day. Although, you know, I was thinking a couple of nights ago that theatre, television, film and radio always need character actors. They are the backbone of acting after all. Not everyone's cut out for the big stuff, the leading parts. You should think about character acting, Alison. You'd be great at that.' Jane said the last sentence slowly and carefully, looking into Alison's reddening eyes. The women held stares for a few seconds.

'Ally, come over here, my love,' Nicholas said. He seemed to leap away from the man in the linen suit and hug her in one graceful move. He was clearly more drunk than she was, but all the same, his overt display of affection and warmth thrilled Alison. It made her feel the type of special she had needed all evening and had the wonderful side effect of mutating the smile on the face of Jane Pritchard, who couldn't conceal such flagrant jealousy and quickly moved away to join a large group of students who had started a Shakespearean drinking game.

'You were stupendous. You were so beautiful and good. You were so good every fucking night, Ally. I wanted to cheer you every line time… I mean, every time you said a line.'

'You weren't too bad either, Romeo, my Romeo. Who was the guy in the suit?' Alison said and began to kiss Nicholas on the neck. He smelled of aftershave and sweat and she wanted to take him to bed immediately.

Nicholas looked to one side.

'He's an agent, with a big firm I think. He gave me all sorts of hyperbole about how great I was and will be. I believe he gave me a card or something and asked me to call him. Who knows? These guys get paid to draw impressionable young idiots in. He probably says that kind of bollocks every night of the week. It doesn't mean anything really.'

'Wow, that's fantastic, Nick. You have to call him. He could be your ticket to the big time.'

'Yeah, well, when I'm done learning how to really act, then maybe I will. Come on, let's get really fucking hammered, eh?'

The three weeks after Romeo and Juliet were blissful to Alison and she often looked back on those twenty-one days as a timeout from the awful truth about life: as hard as you try to preserve moments of pleasure and happiness, or even the images of those moments in your memory, time always erodes the good.

Nicholas was so attentive to her needs: breakfasts in bed; walks hand-in-hand in the autumnal parks of London; introducing her to his parents. His father was powerfully intelligent and his enthusiasm for the arts was contagious. Alison hoped she would be with Nicholas for the rest of her life and watch him grow into the kind of man his father had become. Nicholas's mother was a delight to talk to about acting. Alison confided in her about Jane Pritchard's single-minded attitude to becoming a star and how Alison guessed she would do anything to see her name in lights.

'She'll probably fail in her first choice of ambitions, most of us do,' Nicholas's mother said. There was no sign of ennui in the older woman, just a knowing smile.

Alison held back her fears about Jane stealing Nicholas away. That was a very private fear, deeply embedded in her head every waking moment, and increasingly amplified when they were back at drama school.

Nicholas was like a dream-lover in those three weeks. He had lost the intense commitment of becoming Romeo. His body seemed looser, more at ease with itself, and he talked about them spending Christmas together. Alison was deeply in love, but she never found the courage to tell Nicholas as she had planned to.

The next production was announced in October: A Moon for the Misbegotten by Eugene O'Neill. Alison hadn't heard of it. The only O'Neill play she knew was Long Day's Journey into Night.

The production required three actors: two men

and one woman.

Alison added her name to the audition request list and Nicholas borrowed her biro to write his name down.

'Be great if we worked together on this. Do you know the play?' he said.

'No, I'm going to buy a copy.'

'It's about desperate lives, secrecy and deceit. The juiciest parts are Josie and James. They have an odd romance. It's so very different to the Shakespeare work. Let's learn the lines and rehearse together, eh?'

'Sure. Yeah. Sounds fantastic.'

Alison's enthusiasm for memorizing her lines and rehearsing the role drained away as soon as she saw the elaborately red-inked name of Jane Pritchard standing out like a detonation of intent, right at the top. Hers was the first name there and more than likely, after her success with Juliet, she would be first choice again.

The play stumped Alison from the beginning. She couldn't immerse her experience into Josie, because she couldn't imagine ever being that kind of person. It wasn't anything to do with differences in vernacular or character traits. She just wasn't interested in the part, but she wanted it and needed it. She had to get it to stop Jane Pritchard invading her world again and again.

Nicholas landed the role of James. Alison had watched his audition and become entranced by the sheer physical force of his words and movements. He seemed to have the instinct and ability to transform into whichever part he took on. Alison read the play aloud with him lots of times and he seemed to her to be the only actor who could be James; that Eugene O'Neill had a premonition that one day a brilliant young actor would read his text and know he was the character. Alison knew she would probably never be that good, and she didn't really mind because she had Nicholas in her head, her heart, her life. Surely there was nothing wrong with the vicarious thrill of watching his performances and imagining her own efforts matching his.

'Okay, Alison. Would you begin, please,' Miss Mullins shouted out, again leading the audition process. Alison found herself, again, with Nicholas at her side as the lead actor, his smile willing her to succeed, and Jane Pritchard, literally, waiting in the wings.

'And I didn't hit you, or you'd be flat on the ground. It was only a love-tap to waken your wits, so you'll use them,' Alison said, in her own voice and accent. The words sounded clear and defiant to her, exactly the blend Nicholas had recommended. She knew she had given a good show. The actor before her, Rachel Madison, had used an American accent and mangled certain words in the process. Alison had watched Miss Mullins throughout that audition, her face tight and disdainful, and decided against taking any similar chances.

'Thank you, Alison. That was really very nice.'

Nicholas smiled warmly and gave her a double thumbs-up as if he knew she had nailed the role beyond question.

Jane Pritchard walked past Alison, without acknowledging her, out into the middle of the rehearsal room and shook Nicholas's hand with both of hers as if they were good old friends. She whispered something in his ear and they both laughed. Alison felt a surge of anger through her arms and hands. She wanted to rush at Jane and leap on her head, tear clumps of her hair out and pummel those eyes into swollen bulges.

Her head started to throb. Were they laughing about her audition just finished? Surely that was ridiculous. Nicholas loved her and he knew she was still in the room. But the proximity of their faces to each other, the little comfort zone of familiarity they had created as a lead pair in Romeo and Juliet seemed to have continued and possibly grown into something that couldn't be ignored or washed away so easily as scoring a part Jane desired.

Alison sat and watched Jane audition with Nicholas. She watched Miss Mullins again too. By the end, she knew, just as she had done with the part of Juliet, that Jane had defeated her.

The three weeks came to an end when Nicholas said he was too tired to see Alison that evening. Nicholas had never been too tired or ill to spend time with her before and he sounded different on the phone. It was the change in cadence of someone's voice that provokes memories and analysis for years to come: distant, oblique, withholding; conjecture that could drive a person insane.

'I'll text you later or call in the morning. Is that all right? I'm feeling a bit fluey too. I think I'll have an early night,' he said.

'All right. Okay. Well, if you need anything at all just call or text. Bye,' she said, trying to hide any sign of a 'frown' in her voice as her mother always called it.

'Bye.'

Alison sat and tried to read. She played her favourite playlist and drank some wine, and then she had a bath and tried to meditate.

All she could see behind her eyelids was Jane Pritchard in rehearsals as Josie – she had won the part of course – prancing around the stage without any subtlety. The director had described Josie as a character full of false energy and bravado, desperate to enable the men around her and find love. Jane had taken the description as a starting pistol to unleash her full range of emotive face-pulling, expressive limb-flailing and voice projection. And the director, Mister Jennings, seemed to love her interpretation. The class had to watch each rehearsal, make notes from the stage directions and give detailed and, worst luck, objective opinions on the performances.

Nicholas was the polar opposite in his characterisation of James. He played the man as a successful failure: an oxymoronic twist in the part that Nicholas had mined and taken as the foundation block. He was calm and thoughtful. He smiled and nodded, and delivered his lines with a slight drawl, using every syllable as if he wanted to create some kind of avenue to hope.

'He's amazing, Al, but it must be weird to see him always pairing up with Jane,' Rachel Madison said, during one of the last class rehearsals.

'Why? It's just acting. It's not like they're…anything at all,' Alison said. She smiled at Rachel and wondered whether anyone else, perhaps everyone, had noticed the emergence of a Nicholas/Jane trend. She knew it really didn't mean a thing. However long Bitchard had Nicholas for during rehearsals, Alison had him for longer in bed. That was what counted. That was what Prickhard wanted, and that made Alison grin.

Alison got out of the bath, dried herself quickly, got dressed and left her flat. She bought a cold/flu remedy and some high-strength Vitamin C soluble tablets at a supermarket, and then caught a bus to Nicholas's flat. Living and studying in London was great for the array of social possibilities, but the lack of a real campus, with students spread across the capital in shared houses and flats, made for some drawn-out travel plans.

She got off the bus a stop earlier than usual. She was feeling guilty about her plan now. Nicholas had said he wanted to rest and she had, impetuously, decided to ignore his wishes and foist her idea of helpful on to him. How would he react? Would she ruin the perfect time they had just spent together? Would her behaviour be perceived as odd and push him into Jane's arms? She hesitated, looking around at the night traffic. She considered getting back on a bus and just keeping the cold/flu items for herself.

'Jesus, Alison, come on. Make up your mind,' she whispered.

A light drizzle began coating her face and the damp seemed to galvanise her decision. She would write a note to him and push the medicines through the letterbox. His flat was on the ground-floor, next to the front door, and he was sure to find the care package in the morning. In that way, she would look caring and thoughtful, not at all the creeping stalker she was beginning to feel like.

She wrote: For my lover, in the hopes you quickly recover. Love Al xx She knew the rhyme was corny, but she was certain he would smile at it. She wedged the paper into the remedy box and began to walk towards his flat. The first thing she noticed was a sliver of light coming from a gap between his curtains. The curtains never met in the middle; whoever made them had obviously ignored the basic principle of measuring the bay windows first.

She ducked down behind the wall just in front of his window and scurried up the path. She deposited the package through the letterbox as quietly as she could and then scurried back. She was satisfied with herself, about to blow a kiss at the lighted sliver and walk back to the bus stop when she noticed something that stopped her breathing.

Hands. More than two hands. Hands and a barely visible sign of someone's back moving. She ducked down again and found herself crawling from the path to a position just beneath Nicholas's windowsill. She gripped the wet sill with one hand and then the other, and slowly lifted her head up as if she were in a First World War trench, trying to avoid having her skull blasted in two by machine-gun fire.

Tears came quickly and the urge to scream harder than she could have imagined began to flood her mind. She clamped her mouth shut and slapped a sodden hand across it.

All the worst fears about her love and its worth had come to fruition; her open heart gifted to a man she had always felt less than, and in awe of, but completely devoted to beyond any previously felt emotion. And there she was, on her knees in the rain, watching everything that had felt good in her life being vividly destroyed.

Nicholas was fucking Juliet; fucking Josie; fucking Jane Pritchard.

Ben

Ben texted and called Stephanie at least fifteen times within the first twenty-four hours of her flight home to Paris. She didn't reply and he, a fool in love for the first time, didn't take the hint.

Her answering service was, of course, in French, and his foreign language skills were lamentable enough for him to wonder if he was dialling, and re-dialling, the wrong number. Surely that was a lot more likely than the alternative: that she had fucked him in the hotel room and then fucked him again as soon as her plane left the ground. Why would she do that?

'What do you reckon, Dave?' Ben said, sipping a pint in the local pub and staring into his best friend's face, looking for any sign that he was being paranoid about the French brush-off. Why would David know the finer details of Stephanie's motivation? He was just getting serious about his new girlfriend, Sarah, and had reached the stage of believing she was beyond reproach in all things. How could he empathise?

'Honestly, I don't know. But it does seem as if she's

either not answering her calls and texts because she's busy, with this big family event you mentioned, or… well, because she doesn't want to answer your calls and texts. Sorry, mate, but then I'm guessing you knew that already.'

Ben had thought about everything David said in advance. He knew the reason for the communication shutdown was probably based on the latter reason. Perhaps it was standard practice for Stephanie and other models to get it on with whomever they fancied and then drop them in the bin like a used condom. Who would turn down sex with a model after all?

'I'm such a dick. I never usually let myself get in so deep, so quickly, with women. I can't believe I fell for her. What would she have done if I'd taken up the offer to go to Paris with her?'

David smiled and sipped his drink. 'Ben, she's a gorgeous, intelligent woman. What were you supposed to do? She was probably counting on you being British and thinking of work first.'

'Which I did. Jesus.'

A month passed by. Stephanie didn't call or text and Ben found himself deliberately avoiding eye contact with any of the female models in the studio. He worked hard and began to walk the streets of London on his days off with his camera, a new Nikon 3100 digital Michael recommended.

Michael Garland also loaned him two retrospective photography collections by Diane Arbus and Nan Goldin.

'I can see you want to shoot real life a hell of a lot

more than fashion life,' Michael said.

Ben looked for the unusual and inane in everyday scenes: homeless people with interesting, handwritten begging signs; mis-matched dogs and owners; and individuals who stopped for a moment, their faces rendered in some expression that reminded Ben of the front cover image for Sartre's Nausea, the one which had drawn him towards photography in the first place. He wanted to dive into a collection of his own ideas – new images, new thoughts – to forget any residual hurt he still felt about the Stephanie affair.

'Very slick, mister camera man,' said a voice behind him.

Ben expected a drunk or some other kind of drug-addled body to be pointing an accusing finger his way as he turned around. He was very pleasantly surprised to find the complete opposite: a young woman, eating a sandwich on a bench a few feet away, dressed in expensive black clothing. As much as he hated to admit it, he had become familiar with the world of fashion and could immediately tell the difference between designer labels and high-street imitations. She was smiling at him in a way that seemed to say, 'Come over here and sit down.' And so he did.

'Why "slick"?' he said. He didn't look at her. Instead, he faffed with his camera, deleting two shots.

'I've been watching you. I've seen you here before. You take a lot of photographs and you never ask for permission. I think you may have taken me recently,' she said. 'Are you a spy?'

'I wish. I'm just a humble wannabe photographer

trying my hand at something that interests me,' he said, and then he allowed himself to look at her, wondering for a hesitant moment if she would disappear like Eurydice in the gaze of Orpheus.

'Are you a professional or just a voyeur?' she asked, biting into her sandwich. Her eyes were a sparkling green. Ben didn't want to ogle her like a creep, so he looked ahead and tried to think of something unpretentious to say. He couldn't talk about Sartre or Orpheus, that was for sure.

'I work for a fashion photographer and I'm learning the trade. But I really don't want to shoot models for a living, although there are a few I would like to shoot.'

Ben closed one eye and exhaled, embarrassed at his own joke, but it got a laugh.

'That bad, eh? I'm Helen.'

'Ben. Nice to meet you, Helen. I do recognise you. I was just being cool, or trying to be. I took your photograph last week.'

'Did it come out well? Did you get my best side?'

Helen turned her head the other way and sucked her cheeks in, then smiled again.

'You looked spectacular. Would you like to see it?'

"Spectacular" and an offer to meet you again, wow. You are a smooth operator, Ben. As I said, very slick.'

'That's me, slick Ben.'

'I would love to see my picture, Ben. Do you have a mobile with you? I'll give you my number.'

'Your real number, I presume?' Ben asked, thinking of his last kiss with Stephanie and her smile as she walked away towards the departure area. All lies.

'Of course. Who gives out a false number?'

The first date with Helen was like meeting an old friend; they already had photography in common.

'Any hidden cameras I should know about?' Helen asked, looking pretend-nervous, kissing Ben on the cheek as she sat down. They had picked out a neutral space – an Italian restaurant in Soho. Ben had brought along a small portfolio of his work, including the two shots he had taken of Helen in the park.

'These are good, really good. But, yuck, who ever she is, wow, she is too repulsive for pictures.' Helen held up one of her own portraits and grinned.

'So I want to start putting together some kind of exhibition soon, but it's really hard to find a gallery that will take a chance on a new face,' Ben said. He cut and ate some of his calzone, sipped some wine, and wondered if he was dominating the conversation too much. Photography was all they had spoken about since their original meeting the day before. He didn't even know what she did for a living. The expensive clothing told him she was unlikely to be a student. 'God, I'm so sorry, Helen. I'm so rude. I haven't asked you anything about yourself. I've just rambled on and on about boring photography.'

'That's all right. We have plenty of time, and I like to see and hear passion in what people do.'

'Do you work near the park?' Ben asked. He looked into her eyes again and realised he was avoiding doing so since she arrived. He didn't want to fall in love with her the way he had with Stephanie. He didn't want to idealise another beautiful woman and wait for her to return his calls and texts. He thought about Chet Baker singing,

"I fall in love too easily, I fall in love too fast".

'Pretty near, yeah. I'm a fellow in astrophysics at UCL,' Helen said. She cut a piece of pizza and smiled at him.

'That sounds amazing. I feel like a real bozo now.' Ben took a long drink of his wine and sat back.

'Why?'

'Well, I'm going on and on about photography and art, and there you are, doing something incredible, studying life, the universe - '

'And everything? I know, I know. Douglas Adams was great, eh?' Helen laughed.

'He was, yeah. But really, astrophysics, that's immense. I was always useless, am useless, at sciences. What do you study in particular?' Ben asked.

He was beginning to fall in love, or something like love, with Helen – a kind of rapture perhaps – regardless of any inner voices of experience or wisdom, regardless of David giving him a pep talk before he left for the date: "Just have a good time and relax. Don't take things too seriously. Okay?"

David's girlfriend, Sarah, had given Ben a hug for good luck too. Ben already liked her and was a little envious of David's good fortune to have found such a solid love so quickly. The two of them seemed perfect and were already at the stage of discussing moving in together. Ben had spent the tube journey to Soho wondering where he would live if David moved out.

'Solar flares,' Helen said.

'So, that would be... what?'

'Basically it's energy being released from the surface

of the sun – explosions of sorts.'

'Right, okay. Why do you need to study them?'

Helen laughed again.

'My field of work relates to the impact the flares have on the solar system in general, and what they mean in terms of their speed, size, that kind of thing. It's pretty dull if you don't have an extreme interest in all things stellar.'

'It sounds incredible, truly. I was looking through a book of photographs taken through the Hubble telescope recently and I just couldn't get my head around the colours, the shapes, the whole universal mystery thing.'

Helen reached out and took Ben's right hand.

'Let's pay and get out of here, shall we?' she said. She leaned across the table and Ben met her halfway. They kissed, sat back and Ben asked for the bill.

Two months passed before Ben had to face Stephanie again. He saw her name in the appointments book on Michael's desk and felt a chill run down his spine. He thought about telling Michael he felt ill and was going home. Things with Helen were going so well. They had spent virtually every night together since the Italian restaurant, and although she was doing some research with NASA in Florida at that moment, he felt as if he would be betraying her just by witnessing the mere sight and sound of Stephanie in his universe again.

Then he thought about how things had never been resolved within his own French connection, the way he had been thrown away, and some part of him wanted Stephanie to feel the discomfort of pretending glamour and style and good times in the glare of the studio lights while he lingered on the sidelines with the Champagne bottle and cigarettes, like an epicurean ghost.

He looked at his watch and waited by the front door of the studio. He checked his hair in the round mirror to his right and straightened his collar. He had borrowed a shirt and trousers from the studio's large wardrobe collection. Eventually, he watched Stephanie's car service arrive.

She climbed out, thanking the driver for holding her door open, and walked towards Ben. She was smiling at him, waving and looking relaxed, exactly the way he imagined she wouldn't behave.

'Bonjour, Benny,' she said and kissed his cheek. 'Let's talk after the shoot, okay?'

Ben was about to ask her not to call him Benny and say he was too busy to talk, and didn't have anything to say to her anyway, when Michael Garland appeared.

'Steph, you look even more beautiful than ever. Come this way, darling,' he said. He smiled at Ben and nodded.

Ben followed them in and spent the entire shoot perfecting his level of outrage at her behaviour and his disdain for her laissez-faire attitude. The killing joke/lie he would tell her was she had only ever been a notch in his belt, a trophy lay, and a good dinner conversation piece.

Stephanie obviously had her methods of working. Every time she arrived at the studio she appeared ready, full of confidence in herself, and not because she was beautiful, but because she was a professional. She knew what the cameras wanted and always found a way to capture exactly what the photographer asked for. She laughed easily and seemed to have a fundamental grasp on enjoying life – perfect for fashion shoots. It made her exciting to be around too.

Ben hated the fact that she, at least, was able to switch off any atmosphere his mood might be creating and slip into the moment: her and the lens, the lights and the images. Michael Garland always enjoyed her visits. Ben suspected he knew of the affair between his assistant and the model.

'Fabulous, as ever. Thank you, sweetie,' Michael said, kissing Stephanie on both cheeks when the session was over. 'Ben will call your car. See you again soon.'

Ben and Stephanie looked at each other for a moment. The studio was completely silent.

'I better get changed,' Stephanie said, walking towards the dressing rooms. Ben darted towards her and met her just inside the doorway of the dressing room area. He kissed her hard, stepped back and leaned in again.

'We need to talk, Benny. It's not so simple,' Stephanie said, moving to one side. She smiled, stroked his cheek and walked away to change. Ben thought of Helen looking at the stars in the Floridian night sky, maybe thinking of him and their plans to meet each other's parents soon, which was a big step for Ben. He felt like pond scum. What on earth was he doing? Like a desperate loser, he was kissing the woman who had kicked him out of her life so easily, and now he was allowing her to draw him back into the superficial world where he would always lose.

'I'm staying at The Dorchester. Will you meet me after work, say, six o'clock?' Stephanie said. Her car had arrived. The driver was waiting, holding the passenger door open. Pressure was building in Ben's head. He nodded affirmatively. Stephanie kissed his cheek again. The sensation of her lips on his skin and her perfume almost made him keel over. He smiled and opened the studio door for her.

'I'm in room two twenty-six. Later then,' she said.

The car drove away. Ben was still holding the door. He closed it slowly, diverting his thoughts away from the hellish truth that he was cheating on his girlfriend. He wondered if the way Stephanie had walked in earlier, held court with the camera, pulled him back under her spell, and then left at such a rate, whether that way of life personified the jet-set model way of being. Perhaps, just as F Scott Fitzgerald said that the rich are different, maybe models were different from mortals too. He knew he wouldn't be able to hold on to someone like Stephanie in the long run; that much had already been established from the last time they were together. But the way she made him feel in the moments they did share was unlike real life, unlike Helen or anyone else he knew.

Helen was lovely, funny, clever, interesting and interested in him. She was exactly the kind of woman he should be with; she was exactly right for him. He had fallen in love with her, but life with Helen was real. He would never eat caviar in a five-star hotel bedroom with Helen, or hear stories about various celebrity drug problems, or get offers to fly off to Paris at the last moment.

Ben arrived at The Dorchester at ten to six. He approached the reception desk. He had drunk half a bottle of studio Champagne on the taxi journey and was feeling charged with adrenalin.

'I'm here to see Miss Jaboudon in room two twenty-six. My name's Ben,' he said to the reception-ist. He looked into her face as she called Stephanie's room, searching for any hint of derision: 'This guy! To see a supermodel?'

'Go straight up,' the receptionist said, pointing to the lifts. 'Third floor.'

'Third floor, please,' Ben said to the lift attendant. He was the only passenger and tried not to sway or look into the full-length mirror behind him.

'Thank you, sir. Have a good evening,' the lift attendant said as Ben walked away.

'You too.'

Did the hotel staff talk about the guests and their visitors? Would the lift guy go back to the reception desk and have a good laugh at Ben's expense?

'Benny, come in,' Stephanie said, kissing him on both cheeks. She was fully dressed. Ben had half-expect-ed her to be naked when she answered the door, guid-ing him into the bedroom, and her bed, with her index finger and long red nail, like a beacon of lust. Everything seemed to be shifting into the faintly surreal in his mind. His perception of how things would occur and conclude was muddled. The Champagne had made him drunk. They sat on opposite ends of a large suede sofa. The hotel suite was huge. Darkly varnished wood panels and bright mixtures of flowers seemed to be everywhere.

'I want to explain what happened, Benny. I owe you that. It must have seemed so rude and cruel not to reply to your texts or calls. I guess you thought I was either completely insensitive or dead, eh?' she said.

'Both, I think. Or at least I… I don't know. That was then. I have a girlfriend now. She's called Helen and she's an astrophysics…astrophysicist. She's in Florida and I love her.' Ben said the words quickly. He wanted to appear confident and in control, but he was left with the distinct feeling that he had merely made himself look pathetic to Stephanie.

'That is good for you,' Stephanie said, but Ben was convinced she wasn't really happy with the news. 'Anyway, I want to tell you why I didn't get back in touch - '

'Look, it doesn't matter. I shouldn't be here.'

'Please, Benny. Just allow me ten minutes to get this off my chest, just ten minutes. Okay?'

Ben liked the sense that he was in charge of everything at this point in time. He shrugged and sat back.

'When I got back to Paris, my father and mother met me at the airport and were very excited about something. I assumed it was because I was home after such a long time and we were about to have a big family celebration, but I was wrong.'

Stephanie took a sip from a bottle of water.

'So…' Ben said, deliberately inserting a tone of emerging boredom in his voice.

'So I was surprised, no, I was stunned when we arrived home to find Michel waiting outside the house to greet us.'

'Stephanie, please don't talk to me as if I know these people. You said you wanted to tell me what happened. You need to be more precise. Who is Michel? A man or a woman?'

'I'm sorry. I'm finding it hard to explain and, obviously, English isn't my first language. Michel is a man. He was my fiance.'

'Ah, right. Christ. He was your fiance or is your fiance?'

'Was, definitely was. The thing is we never broke things off properly, officially. He's a doctor with Medicins Sans Frontieres and spends months in Africa. The last time we spoke, he said he wanted me to feel free to see other people, that it wasn't fair on me with him being absent so much.'

'But I can see you still love him.'

Stephanie looked shocked at Ben's blunt statement. She exhaled and sat back, bringing her knees up to her chin. For the first time, Ben thought she looked reasonably ordinary, unglamorous, as if she was a young girl pondering her future, and she looked even more beautiful because of her sudden vulnerability.

'I do still love him, but it seemed impossible for us to be together. He was back in France on leave and had called my father to say happy birthday, and they invited him to the party.'

'Did you sleep with him?' Ben regretted asking the question immediately. It had nothing to do with him and he didn't want to think about the details. He and Stephanie had only shared one passionate night and a kiss that afternoon. 'I'm sorry, that's nothing to do - '

'It's all right, Benny. You have a right to the truth. Yes, we slept together and I told him I want to be with him. I'm going to give up modelling and travel with him. It seems crazy now, but it's what I want. I'm sorry if that's not what you wanted from me. I do feel awful about the way things happened and how I treated you. The time we spent was very lovely.'

'I guess it's a good thing I didn't travel to Paris with you.'

Stephanie rolled her eyes and laughed. 'Oh my god, yes, that would have been so awful for you,' she said.

She leaned across the sofa and hugged him. He kissed her cheek and his lips brushed over hers. And then they were kissing each other hard and long. He lifted her up and carried her to the bed. As he took off his shirt and her bra, he could see out of the tall, wide windows. The night sky was full of stars.

'Why did you need to tell me about that, about her?' Helen shouted. She had packed the last of her personal items – a jumper, two novels and some make-up – and was standing in the doorway of Ben's bedroom. David and Sarah were downstairs. 'Why fuck everything up in secret and then rub my face in it as soon as I get back from Florida. Do you know how much I missed...' She kicked a pair of Ben's shoes across the room.

'Please, Helen, I had to be honest,' Ben said. 'I'm so sorry. I told you about her because I wanted you to know I'm free of any old feelings now. It was just sex. She's gone from my mind and my life. I'm going to quit the studio too, go freelance, do wedding photography on the side to fund my portfolio. I love you.' He had absolutely no confidence in his own words or their worth.

'Oh my good god. Did you really say, "It was just sex"? That is such a lame statement, such typically male reasoning for lying and cheating and being a complete bastard. Just sex? How would you feel if I said I had given blowjobs in the toilets to all the astronauts at the Kennedy Centre? Would that be all right? It would just be sex.'

'I know, I know. The "just sex" comment was ridiculous, of course it was. That's not what I meant. I meant, mean, it was…like an exorcism of something I used to feel – a purge. It was a horrible, intensely stupid and cruel way to behave and I'm sure I don't deserve any forgiveness from - '

'No, you don't, you fucker. You seemed like such a great guy. I had told my mum I was finally in love. You've destroyed any faith I had. I want to…Oh, just fuck off, Ben. Fuck off and die, okay.'

Helen ran down the stairs and then the front door crashed shut. Ben sat on his bed and looked at his bookshelves. He pulled down his copy of Nausea and for a second or two studied the front cover again. His thoughts zipped back to the beginning of his interest in photography. There was a distance between him and the world through the lens. Then he thought about the fact that he would never have Stephanie again. He would never see her smile, unless he came across a magazine photograph of her. Helen had been exactly right for him. He tore the front cover off the novel, ripped it into small pieces, and threw them into the air. Some of them landed on his head and felt like the ashes of his happiness.

David

Where was Ben? David had texted him three times and called him twice, leaving exasperated messages on his answering service. They had made a definite arrangement to meet at the solicitor's office at two-twenty, ten minutes before Sarah was due to arrive. It was two-twenty-five now.

'Ben, it's me again. I…' David stopped talking and pressed End Call on his mobile as he watched his best friend walk into the reception area. Ben was walking and talking with Sarah. Walking, talking and laughing as if they were on a beach and the day had been perfect.

'Hi. Did you get my messages?' David said to Ben. Ben said he hadn't and David shrugged as if to say, 'Ah well, doesn't matter.' But it did matter. He had wanted, needed, some time with his friend, his confidant, the one person in this complete mess he could trust and talk to openly. He had wanted to feel as if he had emotional back-up and yet the worst-case scenario of being left alone – Ben arriving late and with Sarah – had left him feeling like an outcast, an untouchable.

The two men hugged each other – a gesture they had cemented since the earliest days of their friendship. After the hug, David looked at Sarah and wondered if he should try to show her some affection too. What was the protocol in these kinds of situations? Was there one? He smiled at her and nodded. The return expression on her face was akin, if David had been pushed to describe it, to the look a person has when they realise they have trodden in dog shit.

The three of them sat down. Ben and Sarah continued talking about some film they had both seen recently. David thought about the speed of life and its changing patterns. A month or so before, he and Sarah had had sex for the very last time. It was an awkward occasion. Awkward was a considerate description of what had happened. They had arrived home at the same time, something which virtually never occurred. Sarah always stayed a bit later than most to work or go to the pub with colleagues for a quick 'winding down' drink.

David seized the opportunity to follow her upstairs, and as she was about to get changed out of her work clothes he noticed she was wearing hold-up stockings, something she only wore when the weather was very warm and she needed to maintain the appearance of formality. He felt a surge of lust. They hadn't made love for a long time at that point and he had prowled – the only appropriate word, but a word for creeps, he thought now – into the bedroom and put his hands under her armpits to cup her breasts. She had put her hands up and quickly removed his fingers. He assumed she had been shocked and not thinking about any feelings of rejection he might have, and so he had carried on with, what seemed now, his tawdry seduction.

Sarah ended up on top of him, giving out a complete sense of 'doing one for him': lacklustre thrusts; total silence; all over and done very quickly. He found his sexual energy draining away like blood from a severed artery. He realised after they finished, she had kept her eyes closed the whole time. He tried to kiss her but she said she needed to use the toilet urgently.

He wondered if she would have ended up leaving him before or after they were married. If she couldn't even face him when they had sex, before the wedding, how would she cope with the implication of years in the same bed, moving further away from his hands in the night?

He rubbed his forehead and closed his eyes. He wanted to ask her about the sex, her thoughts and feelings towards him in the last days they were together, and whether he was wrong to be feeling the all-encompassing guilt for being the first one of them to crack and go. She was right there, one seat away. They had ten minutes until the contracts were due to be signed. Sarah had re-mortgaged the house and planned on taking in a lodger. David was to receive a pay-off. He had made an agreement that he would have absolutely every last one of his possessions out of the house by the end of that day – another reason for Ben's presence.

Ben and Sarah were still talking about his latest photographic work. He was still plodding along with weekend wedding shoots and trying to launch his own exhibition.

'I think I have enough good shots to self-publish a collection now,' Ben said. It was the first clear sentence David had taken in from either of the other two since they sat down. The office was oppressively hot and his throat felt sore and dry. 'There's a gallery that's willing to take the books if I sort out the boring details regarding the layout, wording, all of that.'

'That sounds brilliant. You must be so pleased,' Sarah said.

David realised he hadn't heard her voice for more than two weeks. It was the longest he had gone without hearing it since they met so many years ago. She sounded excited and happy. He felt resentful of that. He wasn't happy or excited. He was hot, flustered and angry with his best friend's lack of interest.

'So you've really got to pay for the books to be printed yourself?' he said to Ben.

'Yeah well, sometimes you have to kick-start the process. There's a recession on, mate. People just aren't publishing art books like they used to.'

'Why would people buy the books if there's a recession on? Isn't it just a waste of your money?' David knew he was being rude, thoughtless and unsupportive, and he didn't care. He'd had enough of the character part he had been playing since the day he walked out: 'Quiet, feeling-bad-about-it-all David'.

'Well, jeez, Dave. Thanks for the support, mate. People with money, those who always have money, love to buy quality art. If you put the books in the right gallery they will come. But I'll remember not to send you a complimentary copy, eh?' Ben said. He laughed. And so did Sarah.

David didn't laugh. He sat and stewed in his resentment. What the fuck is Ben playing at, he thought, getting here late with her, using me as a comedy gimp in front of her. It's almost as if he's flirting.

Before David had a chance to think of a reply for Ben – a reply that wouldn't open a rift between them but would let his friend know he was deeply annoyed with him – the receptionist walked towards them.

'Would you like to come with me, please,' she said.

Sarah walked ahead, making sure she stayed next to the receptionist. David glanced back at Ben as he followed. He raised his eyebrows at his best friend, trying to load and fire off a questioning stare as if he were an actor in a silent film imploring another person, 'Why? What's going on with you?'

Ben gave him a thumbs-up and nodded. David found an answer in his eyes. He was there for support after all.

David sat down on a chair next to Sarah in front of the solicitor's desk. Sarah moved her chair a few inches away from his. He began to think that Ben had been playing the eternal diplomat with Sarah, placating her with small talk about films and photography, making her feel better in the short term about the horrendous situation she was facing: a life alone, living with a lodger – a stranger.

Ben was that kind of person, always looking out for his friends. David couldn't help but feel sorry for

Sarah. She probably assumed Ben was in her corner and David the one out on his own. He smiled and breathed out.

'So you, David, will receive the payment into your bank account within five working days, and by signing these declarations you are turning over the deeds and mortgage solely to Sarah. Is that all clear?' the solicitor said.

David nodded and signed the five relevant legal pages next to the crossed lines. He passed the forms to Sarah and she signed too. There was no small talk in the office, just a sense of formality and the cold, hardened truth. This was the conclusion of the separation. Their relationship was dead and they had just laid it to rest.

Sarah handed the forms to the solicitor, thanked him and walked out. David tried to smile, but he felt a sudden dive in his mood, shot down and spinning towards the ground. Everything is shit, he thought. He followed Sarah back out to Ben.

'So I was saying to Sarah that we should follow her back to your house - her house. Sorry guys,' Ben said. He winced and looked at both of them. Sarah patted his arm and said it was an easy mistake to make. 'The house, and get all of your bits and pieces packed right away. Does that sound okay with you, Dave?' Ben tried to sound upbeat about his suggestion, as if he had put forward a fabulous idea that might involve hours of hedonistic pleasure.

'S'fine with me,' David said. He looked at his hands. They were trembling. He thought of the word tremulous remembered from a song by The Smiths and felt nauseous about this last visit to his home.

'Great, let's get it over and done with,' Sarah said. 'See you back there, Ben,' she added, as if David had signed away his existence as well as the house back in the solicitor's office. Wouldn't she even acknowledge him now?

'Would you drive, mate?' David said when they reached his car. 'My hands are shaking and I feel pretty grim.'

'Sure. I'm really sorry about all of this, Dave. You must feel gutted.'

'I do. But let's remember, I did gut myself. I'll be all right when I finally leave the house. Thanks for all your help, Ben.'

The two men didn't talk much on the drive back. Ben hadn't driven a car for three years. David knew he was concentrating on the traffic ahead.

David stared at the road he had lived on for years. The houses around his own were familiar with their distinctively painted windowsills adorned with plastic boxes full of flowers. The well-swept gutters and freshly painted streetlights made him paranoid for a second or two that the neighbourhood was getting clean after the scourge (him) had left town.

'Right. Why don't you get straight into the loft and start packing up, and I'll have a quick chat with Sarah, try and make her feel better about our short-lived invasion. When you're ready for a helping hand to lift and carry, I can come up. Does that sound all right?' Ben said. David was happy to go along with any plan and be told what to do. He felt numb and clueless.

Ben knocked on the front door. David stood a few feet behind him and thought about his last night in the house when Sarah had stayed with her parents. He wondered if she might confront him with the vodka and the white chocolate, lead him to the stain on the carpet like a bad dog, and scream poisonous admonishments at him about what a devious lowlife he was and how much she hated him, and that she wished him a forthcoming terminal illness.

'Come in, Ben,' Sarah said. She was smiling, but she only had eyes for one person. David closed the front door and walked up the stairs, pulled the cord for the loft ladder and then leaned over the banister for a moment to catch some idea of what Ben and Sarah might be talking about. He couldn't hear a thing. They must have closed the lounge door, he thought, and trudged up the unfolded ladder.

There really wasn't any packing to finish. David quickly realised Sarah had been in the loft and completed the task for him, but he wasn't willing to just call Ben up immediately and leave like a bad smell. He didn't want to play mind games and create an argument. He just wanted to say good-bye: a few minutes of communion with the bricks and mortar before he vanished. He sat down on the warm flooring panels and closed his eyes tightly.

'Do you want tea, mate?' Ben's voice broke the silence and stillness around David.

'No, thanks. I was thinking of getting the boxes down now.'

'Sure. Let me tell Sarah and I'll help you.'

David took one last look around the loft and listened as Ben walked back to the foot of the ladder.

'Okay, let's have the first one,' he said. David was jealous of the carefree tone in his friend's voice. Perhaps he had met a new girl; he must remember to ask later.

'Thanks, Ben,' David said, as the last of his boxes was wedged into a side space of the boot.

Seven boxes, David thought. Seven isn't much to show for building a life, but he didn't say anything to Ben about his melancholy. He guessed it was probably writ large on his face. He had taken a lot of Ben's time across the previous few weeks in the immediate aftermath of leaving Sarah and then in the post-mortem: the how and why and where now. It was a drawn-out grieving phase, which moved onto the guilt part of his new life – the guilt tied up in his desire for the best in Sarah's future and how he had hurt her, but also in his lack of faith in his own future with Alison.

'I mean, I hardly know her at all. When I decided to leave I had the strongest feelings for Alison. I walked around the house one evening when Sarah was out and I knew I had to go; I had to leave and start a new life. I was certain, am, mostly, certain it's with Alison. But what if I'm wrong and I spend the rest of what could be my long life regretting my decision?'

Ben looked at his glass of whiskey and breathed out heavily.

'It's done now, Dave. That's the cold truth of it. You can't ever go back.'

David knew Ben was right about that. Sarah

hadn't spoken to him at the solicitor's office, in the house or as he left with the last box. He momentarily caught her eye as she was closing the lounge door. He wanted to say something, a parting word or two that would travel across years and be remembered as the perfect closure-exchange between a separated couple, something they might even learn to cherish. She had reflexively started to smile and then stopped herself, shooting him the type of blank see-through stare that a person might expect from someone who has absolutely no knowledge, interest or experience in the thing they are observing. It was a stare that chilled David and he knew, as much as he might try over the coming years to forget that damn stare, he never would.

'Aren't you getting in?' David asked Ben, as he opened the driver's door.

'No, no. I said I'd stay and have a chat with Sarah. She's in a bad way, you know, I just want to make sure she'll be okay. You're going straight to Alison's, right?'

'Yeah. Okay. Listen, Ben, thanks again for everything. You really are a great friend. I know I keep saying that, and I really know I'm labouring this sad-sack routine, but you've been amazing. I feel loads better, less of a complete bastard, knowing you're looking out for Sarah too.'

The two men hugged a final goodbye and Ben waved off the car. David watched his friend re-enter the house. He smiled briefly and then swallowed hard. He was soaked in envy.

David parked his car next to Alison's and looked out of his window, over the well-tended communal gardens of the flat-complex, and in through the group of four large square windows of Alison's lounge. She lived on the ground floor and David hadn't decided yet whether or not he liked the feeling of being exposed to any and every passer-by. It was her home. He had a vague plan, perhaps in a month or two, to suggest they moved to a new place and build their own home from scratch.

He was just about to step out of the car and take the boxes to her front door when he caught sight of Alison talking to another man. They were both seated on her sofa, one at either end, drinking tea and looking very serious in their conversation. His first reaction was panic, as if he was an alien and the rest of the denizens of the complex would appear imminently with fire-lit torches, chanting: 'Get him! Get the interloper, Alison groper, ex-girlfriend moper, all-round no-hoper, get him!'

They would chase him to the edge of town where they would stone him. Then he felt angry and frustrated. Alison knew he was coming. He called her forty-five minutes ago and said he was en route. Why would she invite another guy in on such an important afternoon?

Did he have to wait in his car now? Should he knock on her front door as planned, pretending he hadn't seen the actual interloper sipping a cuppa on the sofa?

'Hey, here I am!' he could say to Alison as she opened the door. Then he could fake surprise at the presence of the visitor and make them both feel the onset of discomfort. The other man would glug down the last of his beverage and depart.

Through all the possibilities in his next move, the one question that stood out and demanded attention, demanded an answer, was: who is that guy with Alison? David slowly closed his car door again, even wincing at the click of the catch. For some reason he felt compelled to stay as quiet as he could and slid down in his seat, furtively watching the two of them talking. He recognised the other man as Alison's ex-boyfriend, Ian. He knew that for certain – confirmation as welcome as a kick between the legs – because the first time he and Alison had made love in her flat, there were still a few photographs of her and Ian on bookshelves and by the telephone.

Then the tension in the flat suddenly shifted. Things became animated. Alison was shaking her head, clutching her face, and Ian was up on his feet, pacing back and forth. David guessed he was trying to convince her to take him back. Watching the other man implore and argue made David want to get out of the car, run to the windows – perhaps dive through the glass – and save his new love from whatever was making her so upset. Surely being there in the room with her, a supporting voice, had to be better than waiting?

But he couldn't move. Something compelled him to watch events unfold from afar, as if he were catatonic, going over the worst moment of his life over and over again, his eyes unable to close or move, only focused on the repeating disaster.

Over half an hour passed. David checked his watch obsessively, as if there would come a moment, a decisive point, when he would have to make a move towards the flat; when Alison might realise he hadn't arrived, and that his apparent tardiness and disregard for her feelings might tip the scales of love in Ian's favour.

'Come on, come on,' David whispered hard through his teeth. He pulled his mobile phone out of his jacket to text Ben, but stopped after a few words, remembering his friend had stayed behind at the house to counsel Sarah.

David breathed in, and out. He decided to be a man for a change. If he had to take a few punches and kicks from Ian, so be it. The poor sod was being dumped and he deserved to face and punish the other guy. Alison might even see David's courage in the face of adversity as an act of total love and bravery. It might be something that became her enduring memory of him.

'Right, let's go,' he said to himself, realising immediately he was attempting the psychological task, and lie, of feeling part of a personal army, a group of many Davids who could take on anyone, anywhere.

Then he crumpled himself down into his car seat, feeling squashed flat in his momentum, the air let out of his courage. Ian was walking across the car park, opening the door of his Renault and, within seconds, slammed it shut and sped off. David caught a quick glimpse of his opponent's face. Rage, frustration and bitterness were the three words that came to mind.

So Alison had finally broken the ties to him. She had let him down and put him in her past.

There was a new problem for David. How long

should he wait now? If he arrived within a few minutes of Ian leaving, it would be obvious he had, at the very least, seen the ex-boyfriend rush off. If he waited in his car much longer, Alison might see him there or begin to wonder why he hadn't called or texted to say he would be late.

David pulled his mobile phone out again and typed in a short message: Traffic awful. Be there soon. Luv u xx

He sent the text and looked over at Alison's lounge again. She wasn't in the room anymore and he was thankful for that. She usually left her mobile phone by the sofa. The time advantage might allow his text validity.

He waited ten more minutes and then got out of the car. He stretched and yawned. His heart was pounding, his face flushed and his armpits damp from the stress.

He went to the boot of the car, opened it and picked up a single box. Then he put it back. The fact he knew Alison would still be upset gave him options: he could arrive slightly heavy-handed with many boxes and the Champagne he had bought, full of new-life-to-gether grins; or knock quietly, pretend to be surprised to find her sad, and offer her open arms of love and bring the boxes in later when the setting was more appropriate. He decided on the second idea. There wasn't really any competition.

David breathed in and out, popped his head forwards and backwards a couple of times like a pigeon, and walked towards the flat.

118

He stopped outside Alison's front door, looked through the lobby windows to make sure Ian hadn't come back for one last try at convincing Alison he was the better man for her, and then he rang the doorbell.

Alison answered quickly. Her face looked ashen, full of grief and worry.

'Hi,' she said. 'Come on in.'

'Hello,' David replied. He kissed her cheek. It felt cold and damp. The skin was a bit salty from dried tears. 'I sent you a text saying I was running late, terrible traffic today. Things just seem to have -'

'I didn't get the text. I've been... David, we need to talk about something really important. Would you like a cup of tea?'

'Do I need a strong one for this talk?' David asked. He was attempting to be jovial, but the atmosphere and the look on Alison's face made him wish he had kept his bad joke gagged and bound in his head. 'Tea is great, thanks.'

As Alison boiled the kettle and collected a box of teabags, David noticed two used mugs in the kitchen sink. He wanted to say something to break the painful silence: 'I know you're going back to Ian. Well that's great, that's really fucking dandy for me. I've just walked out on my entire life for you, and now, after tea and a chat with Ian, I'm history!'

Instead of the grand speech, he smiled at Alison and walked into the lounge to look around for the photographs he had remembered of his predecessor. They were gone and that gave David the slightest boost in his confidence.

He didn't hear Alison come into the lounge, and turned around quickly as she laid the tea mugs at either end of the sofa. He wondered whether perhaps Ian had returned and was watching him on the pensive sofa.

'Are you all right?' David said. 'You look very… worried, upset -'

'I'll be honest with you, David. I've just been speaking to Ian, my ex-boyfriend. He was here earlier, about fifteen minutes before you arrived,' Alison said. She didn't make any eye contact. Usually she gazed at David when they were talking.

Well she's being completely upfront, he thought, but that doesn't mean it's good news.

The silence in the lounge hung heavy as they drank their tea, as if a notification of death had arrived.

'Was he here to collect the last of his things?' David asked finally. He tried to sound casual, with the cadence of a man who didn't have a care in the world.

'No. Well, yes and no. He did take some things, but the reason he was here in the first place was because I called him last night with some news… a problem. I… I don't know where to begin. This is so hard for me to say. I know it will probably screw up everything between you and me, and I really want to make a go of our relationship.'

'Alison, what is it? What's going on?'

'I'm pregnant.'

David felt his stomach drop. His hand, holding the tea, began to tremble. She was pregnant. Was it his? That was idiotic thinking. It was Ian's. That was why he was in the flat. That was why he had been summoned.

Did she want to get back together with her actor-ex?

David's head was throbbing with fast-forward scenarios. He closed his eyes and shouted in his head: 'Shut the fuck up!'

'So, you're pregnant. It's Ian's baby, I'm guessing, supposing?'

'Yes.'

'Why was he here? What can he say or do now? Do you want him back? Shall I leave? What -'

'David, listen, I love you. I have fallen in love with you. I needed to tell Ian about the baby. We were with each other for a long time and he deserves to know. But, but, that doesn't mean you and I can't be together. I want to be with you. The question is, do you want to be with me and another man's child?'

Do I? David asked himself loudly. The voice in his head was shouting the question over and over, like a judge demanding a verdict on his existence.

'Of course I want to be with you,' he said. 'But there is one thing we could discuss, one option you must have considered already.' He moved closer to Alison, putting his hand on her leg. She put her hand on his.

'What's that?' Alison said. She put her head on his shoulder.

'Well, it's an ugly word and it's not a nice thing to offer as a suggestion either. You could have a termination.'

Alison lifted her hand away from his and sat up. She turned and looked at David. This was no gaze of affection or conversational interest.

'That's your answer to this, to kill the baby? I know

you've left Sarah for the last time today, and you're probably a bit shell-shocked about everything, but for the record, I am not having an abortion.'

'It's just an idea, so we can have a clean break from the past...a new start. I reckon we'll always be stuck in a rut if we have to deal with Ian being around. Would you feel happy if Sarah was pregnant and I was still in her life?'

'You are unbelievable, David. This has all been about you, hasn't it, since the moment we met and started seeing each other? Your break-up, your guilt, your feelings. Now it's all about what's convenient for you and how we can kill a baby to suit your plans.'

Alison was on her feet now, shouting. She was walking up and down the lounge. It reminded David of Ian's pacing.

'It's not killing a baby. It's a foetus. I know it sounds awful. It is awful. I'm not proud of the idea. I just want to be with you. Listen, Alison, I -'

'A foetus is a baby! Can you hear what you're saying? Please just get out, David. Please leave now. Just give me some space. I've had enough of this shit today.'

'But I've got my boxes in the car. I thought we were going to -'

'I don't know what's going to happen. Please give me some space, David. I've had enough. I'm so tired now. You're just not hearing me. Go, please. Now.'

Alison pointed at the front door.

David stood up and breathed out. He wanted to jump up and down and throw his head back like a small child, whining about how unfair it all was. She didn't understand what his day had been like. It wasn't his fault she was pregnant. He put his mug down and walked silently towards the front door.

'I'll call you soon,' Alison shouted out.

'Fine. Goodbye. Get some rest,' he said.

He walked to his car, got in and turned on the engine. He didn't look back at Alison's flat. He pulled out of the car park slowly, turning right, drove for a couple of hundred metres and then stopped under a tall, overhanging oak tree. He punched the dashboard a few times until his knuckles hurt and shouted a nothing-sound until his throat became sore. Then he leaned over and picked up the celebration Champagne bottle from the passenger side foot recess. He uncorked the bottle without any froth explosion and downed three long gulps. He wiped his mouth clean and stared at the road ahead, which seemed endless.

'The very thought of you, the sheer idea of you,' he sang quietly, thinking of Sarah's blank stare earlier and then Alison's rage at him. Then he drank more and more of the Champagne.

Sarah

Sarah got up early and took an hour choosing her clothes on the day she became the sole owner of the house she and David had bought together. She knew Ben was going to be at the solicitor's office and she was determined to treat the event as a preamble to talking things through with him, getting serious about her feelings and not letting any more time pass before she re-started her life. She was determined to pretend, as much as was possible, that David didn't even exist anymore.

She looked at her clothing and sighed. She realised she had become the personification of boring professionalism over the years. Her job had become the focus when ever she went shopping for new skirts or blouses. She didn't seem to own any seductive clothing at all. When she and David met at uni there wasn't any pressure to try and win admiring male eyes with push-up bras or short skirts. No one had any money to spare on anything except essentials and getting drunk at the weekends. They all seemed young and full of energy, and beautiful in their own way – enough for any attraction and desire to just happen.

She was older now, true, but still young and, she thought, pretty enough to capture the attention of lots of men.

But she didn't want lots of men; she only wanted one. She was going to be seeing him this very day – the first time she had seen him since David had left her.

Of course, David would be there too, like a grim reminder of an old mistake made – a living photograph of indiscretion. He was a stain on her soul that she would remove as soon as she signed the house ownership papers. She wanted to make him feel a rush of lust-filled envy and regret when he saw her; make him feel he was missing out on who she was as a woman – the part of her he had taken for granted and forgotten about down the years. She was a strong, beautiful and sexy lady that he would never have access to again. She wanted to remind him – rub his face in – what he had given away.

She looked in her three-way mirror. She had never liked it, but David had insisted they buy it. 'It feels like it belongs here, the same way we do,' he had said as they struggled to find room for it on the back seat of the car and driven it home from the nearest house-clearance centre.

She scowled at the memory. She had fallen for so much of his bullshit when they moved in: how they would have children together and build a sand-pit at the back of the garden. She began to smile, realising she could still have that life, and hopefully with Ben.

She didn't want Ben to feel any discomfort or guilt about David's feelings if they ever did become a couple, but, in the silence of the house at that very moment, there was a part of Sarah's mind that liked – loved, adored – the idea that David might suffer deep pain in his heart thinking about her and Ben between the sheets of the bed he had chosen.

She applied some lip salve and stood up to take one last look at herself, straightening her shoulders and jutting her chin out slightly. She pushed some hair behind her right ear and licked the end of her right index finger to erase the smallest amount of eyeliner which seemed out of place.

'You look damn good, Sarah,' she said to herself, brushing down her skirt and re-fastening a button for no reason. She took her jacket off the hanger and put it on, looking in the mirrors again and turning her head right and left – her mirror-face, as David always called it. Then she took the jacket back off again. She needed a quick cup of coffee and didn't want to chance any spills before she left.

Her mobile phone beeped a message received sound. She opened it and read: I'm meeting Dave at the solictor's office at two-twentyish. That sounds vaguely specific, eh?! Would you like to meet before that to chat? I feel bad that it looks as if I'm taking sides. I want to be there for both of you. Ben x

Sarah felt her face become hot very quickly and her heartbeat quickened. Ben wanted to meet before seeing David. Was he showing his cards, albeit in a considerate and open way? Yes, absolutely, of course, bring it on. She was desperate to see him before, during and after David. How should she phrase a reply that didn't sound like either a clamorous Gimme-all-your-lovin', or a tepid Ah well, okay, if you insist...?

That sounds really nice. Thanks, Ben. How about Edwards Bar at one-thirty? X

Sarah saw the text leave and sat on her bed to wait for a reply. She tried not to watch herself in the damn three-way mirror, but her peripheral vision kept drifting there. Less than a minute later the reply arrived: Edwards, one-thirty it is. See you there. B x

She had less than an hour. Sweat was building under her armpits. Would she tell him about her feelings before the solicitor's office or after? Why do it at all today? If she told him in Edwards and he, crestfallen, took her hand and told her he could never betray his friend like that and, in any case, didn't think of her in that way, she imagined she might die on the spot, melt into a puddle of humiliated ooze and drain away.

'There is no way I am telling him anything before we've been through the fucking solicitor crap,' she said to herself, feeling a surge of anger towards David again, knowing that any obstacle to her feelings for Ben and their exposure was his fault. Why couldn't he just sign the papers separately and bugger off forever?

It was the solicitor who insisted they both be present: joint undertakings and witnessing was needed. Legal jargon and nonsense, she thought, distracting herself from the increasing anxiety about seeing Ben imminently.

She went to the kitchen and began to boil the kettle,

but soon switched it off again. Her mouth was too dry for coffee. She needed water – lots of water. She filled a glass from the tap and downed it quickly. Then she remembered the blue-label Smirnoff she had recently bought, just sitting in the freezer. She wanted to take a few swigs from the bottle. Dutch courage might mask her inhibitions and allow her the freedom to be herself with Ben, to recreate the intense connection they had shared during their beatific night of dancing.

Sarah ignored the vodka and tidied the kitchen needlessly. It had been neat and shiny for days, the way she liked it, would have always liked it. David had been messy, leaving mugs and plates in the sink, the toilet seat up, never quite moving past student clichés. When they fell in love and first moved in together she ignored his thoughtlessness. She presumed he would mature, realise he was in a shared space with someone he loved, and make the extra effort, but he never did.

Was that a stain? How did it get there? Sarah wondered, looking at the lounge carpet. How had she missed it before? She tried to remember an occasion when the stain might have been created. It wasn't dark enough to be tea, coffee or wine and they never ate meals in front of the television. She stared at the stain, attempting to use its shape and size as ways of determining an incident, but eventually she thought of Ben again, looked at her watch and finally decided to leave the house.

As she closed the front door, she looked up and saw the tiny lettering – S & D – David had painted above the bay window just after they moved in.

Sarah felt a rush of emotion. Tears filled her eyes. Fuck you, David, she thought. She was leaving the house as joint owner for the last time. When she returned, she would own the entire property – with the bank – and, as such, become responsible for the utility bills, the mortgage, and the maintenance of this old place. But, she told herself, walking towards the bus stop, she had recently fixed the floppy hinge on the kitchen cupboard that David always said he would see to. She could take a short-term lodger or sell the house. She was free to choose her future. She wiped the tears away and checked her reflection in a car side mirror. There was the possibility, the chance, the sheer hope, that Ben might eventually move in with her. He might feel squeamish about living in the same house as his friend had, but they could set up together anywhere.

Sarah paid the bus driver, took a seat upstairs and looked out of the window. Today is a new beginning, she shouted in her head. She smiled, watching trees and houses go by.

The last few metres of the approach to the front doors of Edwards felt to Sarah, in terms of stress, like the equivalent of a slow march to death. What the hell was she supposed to say to Ben? How could she take such a huge step with absolutely no real evidence that he felt anything for her at all other than friendship? He would be at the solicitor's office with David later too. If she let her feelings spray out in the short time they had before they met David and he reacted badly to the revelation, appalled by what he might perceive as her callousness, that she could sign away one lover on the same day as she tried to entice another – the best friend at that too – she knew it might be years before she would recover her confidence.

Ben was already sitting in a booth near the back of the bar as Sarah walked in. He quickly saw her and stood up to greet her.

'Hi,' he said.

'Hello,' she said. Sarah immediately tried to read any subtle changes in Ben's smile and the way he kissed her on the cheek, but he always smiled and kissed her on the cheek when they met.

'Coffee, tea, something stronger?' Ben offered.

'Coffee, please… and some water, just tap water, thanks.'

Ben nodded, smiled again, and walked to the bar.

I am in love with you, Sarah thought, watching the back of his head as he ordered the drinks. I am in love with you.

'Coffee and water,' Ben said as he laid a tray on the table between them and distributed the cups and glasses. 'I bought you a Perrier. I hope that's all right with you? I just thought tap water might taste a bit horrible.'

He didn't make eye contact, concentrating instead on where to put the tray.

'That's so thoughtful. Thanks, Ben,' she said.

'So, how are you? I haven't seen you in a while and I didn't just want to turn up at the solicitor's office today as if I'm Dave's henchman.'

Sarah laughed. Now Ben was making eye contact – all smiles and dilated pupils, she thought.

'I wouldn't have thought that. I know this must be hard on you,' she said.

Ben looked surprised.

'Not compared to the two of you. This whole situation must be a bit overwhelming.'

Sarah nodded and rolled her eyes in reply. Then they sat in a few moments of silence and sipped their cups of coffee, as if they knew the opening comments were some sort of prelude. Ben put one elbow on the table and sat up straight.

'You said, in your text, you wanted to talk about something when we met up?' he said.

Sarah hadn't re-read the text for days, always imagining she had more time to think of the most sophisticated responses, and although she knew exactly what she had written, the tone of the missive escaped her memory. She wondered if there was some small phrase which could never be taken back; never leave the receiver in any doubt of the intentions of the sender.

'Well, I…you've always been such a brilliant friend to both of us…David and me,' Sarah said. 'I just wanted to make sure you knew, or felt, that you and I could, and should, stay in touch when all of this is over… the house thing, and David's stuff is moved out.' She picked up her coffee and took a long, uncomfortable gulp, feeling anger along her jawline. How ridiculous did she sound? Brilliant friend! Stay in touch!

Ben smiled and reached across the table. He took Sarah's free hand and squeezed it. She didn't know what to say or do. She wanted to lean forwards and kiss him, but squeezing her hand still wasn't enough to confirm deep feelings.

'It's all right, Sarah. Of course we'll stay in touch. It might be difficult at first, but I'll be around when ever you guys need me.'

The rest of the chat was basic catching-up. Sarah talked a bit about her job and her recent visit to see her parents. She enjoyed the freedom to watch Ben's face without inhibition. He smiled and laughed and seemed to be completely at ease with her, as if they were already a couple, perhaps recounting pastimes of happy events. Sarah revelled in being alone with him, without the awareness that David was at her side waiting for his chance to speak. When had they really stopped listening to each other? she wondered.

Even this gift of time with Ben seemed like a wasted opportunity as the two of them walked the few hundred metres to the solicitor's office, still chatting constantly about nothing much. Sarah felt as if she had been handed the chance to speak from her heart, to say all the meaningful things which had always eluded her with David, and begin the process from where they might start their life together. She wondered if seeing David crushed and alone, and losing his home to her, might set something in motion within Ben's mind and create an illusion of Sarah as a harpy – someone he would never attach his fate to.

'Oh shit,' Ben said, stopping for a moment.

'What's wrong?' Sarah asked.

'I've had my mobile on silent for a while and I've just noticed loads of missed calls and texts from Dave.

I was supposed to be with him a bit before the meeting, you know, to raise his morale. Ah well, I guess I'll have to start when I get there.'

Sarah felt a rush of satisfaction. Ben had chosen her over David. Perhaps that was the sign of a beginning in itself: extrication from the bonds of mere friendship into the silken ties of love.

As soon as Sarah walked through the reception area of the solicitor's office, having confirmed her appointment time and been shown the waiting area, she saw David looking as fiercely nervous as a man guilty of many awful crimes and about to be sentenced to death. With Ben at her side, she felt a wave of confidence which slowed her heart rate and brought a smile to her face, a genuine grin. She didn't care if David saw her that way either. She wanted his discomfort maximised.

'Dave looks grim, eh?' Ben whispered as they opened the glass door to the waiting area.

Sarah smiled at him and raised her eyebrows. She knew it would make a better impression to play things down than to bask in any glorious payback she might be experiencing. Her mother had always told her to take her time enjoying any victory, to reflect on things at leisure.

David and Ben exchanged a few words. David played down his annoyance about Ben's tardy attitude and, thankfully, didn't try to engage Sarah in any chit-chat. Ben sat in the middle and talked about his plans for a self-published book of photography. It was then that David's anger came to the fore. He derided Ben's ideas and made the atmosphere feel noxious.

The receptionist led Sarah and David to the solicitor's office and they went through the boring formalities of signing the house into her sole ownership.

As Sarah half-listened to the solicitor drone on about the legal obligations of the documents, she tried to remember what had drawn her to David in the first place, all those years before. They had been young, at university and willing to take chances. She had once told him, 'I'll love you for as long as you keep me drunk.'

Beyond the cloistered life of tutorials and seminars, essays and exams – the shared frivolity of the long weekends lying naked together, buying Sunday newspapers and arguing about which songs were the best and which gig they should go to – what had kept her with such a cruel individual? Had she become a Pavlovian zombie? Or found herself struck down by some form of Stockholm syndrome?

She made a couple of sideways glances at David and frowned at her guileless attempts to create her perfect life, for all those wasted years. She could have been so much happier with someone else! Someone like Ben. But then, she wouldn't have met Ben without David, and she did love the house she was signing her name to.

Sarah thanked the solicitor and left his office. She and David didn't speak as they made their way back to Ben. What was there to say to him: Cheers for the memories; most of them are crappy. Good luck on life with your fuck-puppet!

Agreement was made about the three of them going back to Sarah's house to finally clear out the last of David's things. Sarah had grown tired of his seemingly endless faffing about in the loft, and she had hastily thrown, shoved and squashed everything she could find of his into seven remaining boxes.

David was obviously wasting time above them as Sarah and Ben continued their chat about nothing much back home in the lounge.

'Shall I make some tea? Would you like a cup?' Sarah asked Ben.

'That sounds great. I'll see if Dave wants one too. Maybe the caffeine will make him move a bit quicker,' Ben replied, rolling his eyes.

Sarah was about to say she didn't want to offer David a cup of anything, but Ben was already on his way up the stairs. He soon returned, relieving Sarah of any need to appear heartless: David didn't want tea. His self-indulgence in the dust motes of the loft had come to an end. The siege was over. The men were moving the boxes to the car and then the house would finally be all hers.

David tried to make some final eye contact with Sarah, a half-smile imbued with god-knows-what. She found herself smiling back, but stopped her facial muscles in their tracks. She would not, could not, live with the thought that he would live the rest of his life falsely imagining that she had forgiven him, that he was all right in her eyes, no damage done. She forced a final look of nothingness, a thousand yard stare of exclusion. She looked straight through him. He was a ghost to her now.

Sarah watched Ben and David through the net curtain. David had obviously assumed Ben was travelling away with him, having opened the passenger door. They had a short discussion of some kind. It was impossible to discern what they were talking about. They hugged and then David drove away. Sarah smiled at the past departing and the future she hoped for, standing in her sights and returning to her front door.

'Hello? Sarah?' Ben called out from the front door.

Sarah opened the lounge door and met him in the hall.

'Hello again. Everything go okay?' she said.

'Fine. Well, he's a bit messed up about things I think, but he'll be all right. Is it still okay if I have that cup of tea?'

'Of course. I'll put the kettle on.'

The two of them walked into the kitchen. The mundanity of filling the kettle, switching it on and listening to it boil was excruciating to Sarah. She wanted to run at Ben, fling her arms around his neck, her legs around his waist, and yell happiness, love, lust and eternity together.

'I was wondering if you would help me move a couple of items of furniture?' Sarah said, thinking out loud on how she could keep Ben in the house for as long as possible. She submerged and bashed the teabags, flipped them into the food compost bin, added some milk and turned to hand Ben his mug – David's favourite mug.

'Sure. No problem. What were you thinking of moving?'

'The sofa and armchairs. I never really liked the way the lounge looked, and there's a stain on the carpet. I don't know where it came from, but I want to cover it.'

'Shall we do it now?' Ben asked. He looked nervous, scratching the bridge of his nose a few times and smiling as if he was hiding something.

'Okay.'

They had a brief talk about the possible, new layout of the room. Sarah deliberately let Ben's ideas seem in line with hers. She wanted him to be drawn to the idea of being comfortable in the house, of living with her. She wanted him to feel differently in this home post-David, renewed in outlook, as if they had just moved into the property.

Ben insisted on lifting the sofa at one end on his own and twisting it to fit an unused corner, and then, after a final confab, he positioned the armchairs at new angles, standing next to Sarah to admire the new interior design. Their forearms touched for a moment and Sarah knew, with the immediacy of the goosebump prickle she felt rising, she would have to tell him how she felt. If she didn't sit him down, right then and there, she might just erupt with a spew of unintelligible verbiage that would, almost certainly, make them both thoroughly uncomfortable.

'Ben, would you mind sitting down for a moment?' she said. 'I really need to talk to you, about me, about… stuff, things…' She felt a warmth grow across her collar bone.

'Yeah, of course. Anything you want to talk about is fine,' he replied, sitting and finishing the last mouthful of his tea.

Sarah sat opposite him. She placed a cushion on her lap for emotional security and cleared her throat.

'I've been feeling...feeling huge changes since David...well, actually, before David said he was leaving. I've been going through a period of thinking things through, and I guess, if I'm being really honest, I don't feel as upset about the break-up as I thought I would.'

Ben sat forward and nodded. 'Well, that's a good thing,' he said. 'It must have been a massive shock. I think you've dealt with things so well.'

'Don't get me wrong, I am angry with David. He lied to me and made me feel like a complete idiot. But that's already in the past and I want to move forward... which is why I'm talking to you.'

'Okay. Good, that's good,' Ben said. He looked nervous again.

'Do you remember, a while back, that night you and I argued about what the word beatific meant?'

Ben smiled and nodded again.

'Yes, I do have a vague memory of feeling like a fool,' he said. They both laughed and all the tension in the room seemed to flatten.

'Do you remember us dancing in that club, after David had dropped out and gone home?' Sarah was speaking very clearly now. She was beginning to enjoy easing out the information in this little game they seemed to have started. Show-and-tell for new lovers?

'I do. It was a great evening. Sarah, I -'

'Please let me finish saying all of this, Ben. Sorry

to stop you, but I really need to get to the end.'

'Sorry, go on,' he said and sat back, crossing his legs and smiling.

'Well...I really have no idea how best to connect that night, David leaving and my continual thoughts about you into one solid thing. But the fact is, Ben... the point of this is...Oh, fuck it. I'm in love with you. I know that might make you feel uncomfortable, even repulsed, because of your friendship with David.' Sarah's voice was speeding up now. 'If you want to tell me to get lost and never speak to you again, I'll understand. But I had to tell you. It's been gnawing away at me for a long time. So anyway...that's it, that's the lot.'

Sarah sat back and breathed out slowly. She swallowed and looked directly at Ben.

Ben stood up and walked into the kitchen. He came back with two glasses of water, handed one to Sarah and sat back opposite her.

'I'm in love with you too, Sarah. I have been for a long time.'

Ben put his glass of water on the floor carefully, stood up again and sat down next to her. He took her glass and put it on the shelf behind their heads in the same spot where there used to be a photograph of David – a picture Ben had taken. Then he kissed her lightly on the cheek.

They both sat very still, holding hands and not speaking for a while. Having finally told Ben she loved him, and having heard him describe the same level of emotion back to her, she had imagined something would happen with immediate force, some unstoppable combustion of love and desire: clothes torn off; their hands so happy with the feel of new skin, unable to find a resting place on any part of the other body; the tumult of lust so overwhelming that their lack of co-ordination, the inexperience of new lovers, would make them drop to the carpet and be wholly consumed by one another.

But there they sat, like a couple in the twilight years of a relationship, beyond the calling of the flesh, just happy to be together, and passion spent with fondness in its place.

That wasn't what Sarah wanted. She guessed Ben might be as nervous as she was, and had been, and that he might still be feeling a surreal shift in his world. Only a short time before they revealed their hearts to each other, he had been helping his best friend pack away his life and watching him drive off. Now he was holding said best friend's ex-partner's hand.

'Are you hungry?' Sarah asked, breaking the silence, and because she was suddenly ravenous.

'Yeah, I am actually. I haven't eaten since this morning.'

'Shall we pop down the road and get a pizza? Or something else?'

'Pizza sounds great.'

As they wandered to the pizza place, Sarah filled Ben in on some neighbourhood gossip: two couples living next door to each other who were thought to be wife-swapping; the guy with a brand new Porsche outside his home, who owned seven other properties on the street; and a student house that was raided for drugs every month or so.

Sarah was trying to speed up Ben's socialisation; increase the pace of normalisation for him. She had a suspicion he knew about the druggy students and the wife-swappers from conversations during drunken evenings with her and David, but she also felt a need to re-introduce him to where she lived and where she hoped he would want to live – with her, and soon.

They ate the pizza and drank the red wine Ben had bought. They talked about Sarah's job. She was under pressure to work evenings and weekends due to an imminent deadline to 'sell' the idea about value for money in the next round of spending cuts.

'So, your book and the gallery that's willing to take it, that sounds fantastic, Ben. You must feel as if things are really starting to take off?'

Sarah glanced at her reflection in the window above the stereo. Night had come and her thoughts were already in the bedroom.

Ben nodded, sipped some of his wine, put the glass down and stood up. He walked around the table slowly, leaned down and kissed Sarah on the lips, slowly at first, and then with passion. He took her hand again, but this time he helped her to her feet before leading her up the stairs.

They kissed at the top of the stairs and halfway across the landing. Sarah couldn't stop herself from glancing up at the loft hatch and, only for a second or two, imagining that David had spent his interminable amounts of time up there creating a portal back into the house, and that he was watching them now, like some hunched weirdo with his hand down his trousers.

They stood next to the window, each having turned a bedside light on, the curtains still open. Usually Sarah would have hated this level of exposure to the outside world, but now she didn't care about anything or anyone else. She was completely present and felt better than she had done for years.

Ben ran one hand slowly up and down Sarah's back, and the other up and down her front. He kissed her neck and hair.

Sarah opened her eyes and for a moment thought she saw a car across the street that looked exactly like David's. She dismissed any curiosity in an instant. There were millions of red Nissan Micras in the world.

'I'm just going to the bathroom,' she said. She kissed Ben deeply again, wanting the dampness of his lips on hers as she walked away.

In the bathroom, Sarah hastily cleaned her teeth, used the toilet and then found a packet of condoms. She looked in the medicine cabinet mirror and moved her hair about a bit. Then she began to smile. The smile grew quickly into a grin.

'Beatific Ben, beatific Ben,' she whispered to herself as she walked back to the bedroom.

Alison

Alison took a month away from drama school in the immediate aftermath of her break-up with Nicholas. She produced a doctor's note detailing depression as a reason for her sabbatical to the student registrar's office three days after witnessing Romeo and Juliet making the beast with two backs. Then she went back to her parents' home and began the process of rebuilding her entire belief system.

The break-up had been a performance in itself. Alison had confronted Nicholas at his front door moments after the horrific realisation that the sum of all her fears was true and being vividly produced. She stood up from her covert position by the damp window sill, felt her jaw lock and her hands open and close in clenches of homicidal rage.

She hammered on Nicholas's window until he pulled back the curtain and looked at her in disbelief, wide-eyed and open-mouthed. Jane was covering her body with his dressing gown.

'You piece of shit. You bastard. I knew you would do this. Why didn't you just dump me and be honest about that bitch?' Alison had screamed the words into

Nicholas's face.

Nicholas stared at the ground, shook his head and began to speak.

'Don't say anything. Don't try to explain your way around this. I suppose this is all part of your method acting? You'd probably like me to believe you were screwing her to get into character? Well you, and that bitch, that crappy bitch in there can both go to hell and rot. Fuck you, Nicholas. Have a nice career and life, and do break a fucking leg.'

Alison ran away from the house. Nicholas shouted after her, asking her to come back, saying he was sorry and that he loved her.

When Alison returned to drama school she showed no visible sign of heartache when Rachel Madison told her Nicholas had left the course, joined a top-drawer theatrical talent agency and already been offered some film and television work. Alison shrugged, sipped some coffee and tried to swallow her feelings with the caffeine.

Her month away had been productive. She had offered her services as an unpaid teaching assistant in the drama department at her old secondary school. Miss Peters was still there.

'Oh, well that is highly typical of actors, of men in general, out to shag anything that moves. I'm really sorry you got cheated on like that, Alison. He sounds like a total arsehole. But it's good to have you back. You'll be an inspiration to these students,' Miss Peters said. Alison felt a warmth in her stomach about being home again, feeling as if she had achieved something, was achieving something, by choosing to act.

When she started back at the Guildhall, Alison had renewed perspective. She could fall back on teaching again when ever she liked and acting wasn't just about the big parts, the methodology and the rivalry. It was about enjoying playing other people, other lives; the range of emotions available in the human heart and mind.

And, yes, if she was being true to herself, she still loved Nicholas and felt a pit in her stomach as she looked around the drama school, at the rehearsal rooms and the canteen. There were always going to be triggers: things to see and hear that would remind her of him. The day would inevitably come when she would watch him perform again, but she was determined not to give in because she had been let down by a narcissist. He had gone and she had the freedom to learn her trade again.

Unfortunately, Jane Pritchard was still there and had, predictably, just bagged the next lead role: Martha in Who's Afraid of Virginia Woolf?

'I reckon she's either Mullins' love-child or she's got something juicy on her in a file, salacious photos or something like that,' Rachel Madison said. 'There is no way her audition was better than Hayley's.'

Alison shrugged off the Jane Pritchard reference. She had made a conscious effort to erase Jane from her memory, avoid talking about her in any way, and asked to be placed in opposing workshops. The Pritchard-avoidance techniques seemed to be working.

There were still moments, however infrequent, when Alison fantasised about cornering her nemesis in a dark and empty rehearsal room, binding her hands tightly to a radiator or something equally immovable, taping over her mouth and then spending glorious hours torturing her with hot pins and depilatory products – how odd she would look without eyebrows – while quoting various soliloquies; those that might evoke a sense of vengeance between foes.

Alison had made a decision to spend more time with Rachel since returning. She seemed to have the right attitude towards the requisite tasks for an actor of study and play.

'There's a party at my house on Friday. You're coming, and no refusals. Okay?' Rachel said.

'Sure, but only for a bit. I'm still not feeling that ready for the 'fun zone' just yet.'

'Yeah, well, listen. You know Ian Cummings? The tall one?'

Alison shook her head, genuinely unaware of his existence up to that point.

'Jesus, Ally. You and Nick really did have your own universe, didn't you?' Rachel said. She began to laugh and then stopped suddenly. 'Shit, I'm sorry, that was so insensitive of me. I didn't -'

'It's all right, honestly. I did have my head up my arse for that time with Nicholas and I didn't socialise as much as I should have done. We're all in this place, this business, together. It's okay.'

'Okay, good. So, Ian Cummings, tall guy. While you were away…and I have to be honest, everyone knew what had happened between you, Nick and Jane.'

Alison shrugged and lit a cigarette.

'So, Ian keeps asking me how you are, whether

you're coming back. He was asking a couple of other people the same questions about you. I told him I didn't know anything, which was true. But when he heard about my party, probably having noticed you and me spending a lot of time together, he asked if he could come.' Rachel grinned at Alison and raised her eyebrows.

'Oh no, Rachel, you didn't say yes, did you?'

'I did, I did. But, listen, he's really nice and sweet. I didn't think it would hurt to have someone at the party who was interested in you. Shall I un-invite him?'

'No. That's completely fine, Cupid. I'm sure we can talk about acting, if nothing else,' Alison said. She deliberately grimaced at Rachel and, for the first time in weeks, felt a lightness in her feelings. It wasn't quite optimism, but she sensed there were other people to meet, talk to, share time with. These were simple realisations that only a couple of months before would have seemed insane, when she and Nicholas were so enraptured by their own lives that they excluded the lives of others.

On the night of the party, Alison felt sick with nerves. What had she been thinking when she agreed to this travesty of fake happiness? She clearly wasn't ready to dance about, either to music or in any kind of conversational dalliance with an 'interested party'.

She picked up her mobile phone and began a text to Rachel – a straight line of honest talking, friend to friend. Then she stopped herself and thought about Nicholas and Jane together, their selfish desires and ambitions. She thought about her time away from the course, the strength she found in teaching, and the effort she was making to move forward. She cleared the text, put the phone in her handbag and finished getting ready to go out.

'That's him, over there,' Rachel said. She kissed Alison on both cheeks and managed to whisper Ian Cummings' position as she pulled back, using a side-glance to confirm things.

'And what exactly am I supposed to do about that?' Alison asked.

Rachel looked directly into Alison's eyes.

'Talk to him, introduce yourself, break through the real fourth wall. I'll tell you what I always do when I'm interested in a guy. I use the methods we've learned about finding characters' motivations, and then I pretend I'm just acting a part; the part of a confident woman who knows what she wants and is going to have it.'

'That's your advice, pretend to be someone else who wants someone she almost certainly doesn't want?' Alison said, and then she laughed, a genuine laugh – the first for a while.

'Well, all right, it's not that well thought out, but give the bit about pretending to be someone else a try. By doing that you can either become Much Ado's Beatrice and be really aloof, or you can switch into full-throttle Juliet without the tragic ending.' Rachel suddenly looked pained. 'Bugger, sorry, Ally, I've done it again, haven't I? I didn't mean to raise the dead like that. Sorry.'

Alison looked quizzical for a few seconds, then realised what Rachel was alluding to: Nicholas and

Jane as the star-crossed lovers.

'As I said, it's all right. I can deal with the past. Listen, let me have at least three or four drinks and then I might speak to Ian Cummings. Is that okay with you?'

Rachel smiled, curtsied and led Alison to the mass of wine and beer bottles in the kitchen.

As the evening went by, Alison found herself laughing and drinking and dancing with Rachel, Hayley Gibson and another young woman she recognised from the Guildhall.

She completely forgot about her original 'mission' for the party.

'Can I get you a refill?' a voice asked Alison over the amplified sounds of Joy Division.

She turned around quickly, immediately feeling dizzy from the alcohol.

'What?' she shouted, focusing on who was asking her the question. Ian Cummings smiled, held up his glass and pointed at hers.

'Drink? Yeah, okay. Red wine, please,' she said. He nodded and walked to the kitchen.

'It is on,' Rachel whispered closely into Alison's ear.

'Shut up and dance, Rach,' Alison shouted. She was drunk and enjoying the feeling. She was shaking loose any inhibition manifested from the break with Nicholas, any sense of not being good enough for anyone to be around.

'Red wine for you,' Ian's voice was familiar this time. Alison took the full glass, swigged half of it down and smiled at him.

'I hear you've been asking after me?' she said.

Ian looked momentarily mortified. He glanced at Rachel.

'Yes. Yeah, I was worried...I mean, I wanted to know whether you were coming back or not. I think you've got a lot of talent. I was just concerned that -'

'It's okay, you know, you can just admit you fancy me.'

Alison smiled, closed her eyes and danced. When she looked at Ian again he was smiling and nodding. I like the look of you, she thought.

Two days after the party, having recovered from the worst hangover of her life, Alison received a text from Ian asking her how she was and whether or not she would be free to meet for lunch in the drama school canteen later that day. She couldn't remember giving him her mobile phone number, but then she couldn't remember large portions of the party night.

She replied that she would love to meet him, sent the text, and then regretted using the word love.

Ian was already waiting at a table when Alison walked into the canteen. He stood up to meet her, automatically putting his hand out to shake hers. She kissed him on the cheek instead.

'I just want to say sorry for all the asking around I did when you were away. I must have sounded like a stalker or something,' he said as they ate sandwiches and drank coffee.

'Don't be ridiculous, it's fine. People have been treating me as if I have a terminal disease since I got back. It was really nice that someone was interested in me because of who I am.'

'Well, I've wanted to talk to you, properly, for a

while now. We've shared a few workshops, but I knew you were with Nick…sorry, I guess you probably don't want to talk about any of that.'

'We can talk about anything you like, go on,' Alison said. She gave Ian her most reassuring smile.

'You were right about what you said when I gave you that first glass of wine the other night,' Ian said. He sipped some coffee.

'What did you say? I'm sorry, I was so pissed. My memories of that night are blurry at best.'

'You said I should just confess that I fancied you. And I do. I know you might not be ready for any kind of relationship yet, but I've liked you, your acting, everything, since we started here. So there it is,' he said.

Alison breathed in and out deeply, finished her sandwich and sat back.

'All right, you've been really upfront and honest with me. You're right, Ian, I'm not ready for another relationship yet. Nicholas really broke me down and I'm dealing with that one day at a time. That doesn't mean we can't get to know each other and see where things go. Is that okay with you?' she said.

'Of course it is. I didn't think I'd get to know you at all. We can take things at any pace and anywhere you like,' he said. 'Would you like some more coffee?'

Alison noticed Jane Pritchard walk into the canteen. They made brief eye contact. Jane looked away quickly and began fussing with the contents of her handbag.

'No, thanks. Tell you what, let's go and get a real drink from the pub across the road.'

Nearly four years later, Alison looked back at the night of the party and regretted having accepted Ian's offer of red wine. She didn't regret every day of the four years, or the fact that she had placed her faith in being part of another acting couple. She also didn't have any great regrets about having spent that amount of time with a man she would eventually decide to leave.

What she most regretted, and felt completely heartbroken by, was that she allowed her ambition and her desire to be a full-time, working, living-and-breathing actor drain away because of being with Ian.

They fell in love after a couple of months of being 'just friends'. Ian proved his love and devotion to her in so many ways. He was a good man. He seemed to value her ideas and her thoughts as much as his own. They both finished drama school full of hope for their performance careers. Alison looked back at that time as one of the best in her life.

Ian got his Equity card first. He landed a three-episode part in a regional soap opera within six months of leaving the Guildhall. It took Alison another eight months to secure her card. She found the 'real world' audition settings intimidating and they quickly drained her self-esteem. Eventually, after two very long auditions for a minor part in a modernised version of Pygmalion – a version which only lasted for twelve shows – she was allowed to join the acting union and finally felt as if she had arrived as an actor.

Their first year as working actors didn't involve much acting. After Ian's soap opera, he tried and failed to find another part for two months and eventually gave in to the cliché of part-time barman duties at an upmarket hotel. Alison took a job working mornings in a sandwich bar and spent the afternoons walking between theatres, looking for open-casting signs, checking audition listings online and scouring the pages of The Stage – she and Ian took turns buying the weekly paper – for forthcoming auditions, extras-needed ads – anything that might keep her within sight of the curtains and lights.

'I think we need a plan, Al,' Ian said. He had just arrived home from work and seemed so excited that Alison assumed, correctly, that he already had a plan to offer her.

'A plan for what?'

'For acting, for us, the future. I was thinking about how we can both maximise our talents and have a better standard of living.'

Ian took off his coat, sat on the sofa and waited for Alison to sit with him.

'I'm all ears, go on,' she said.

'Okay, well, the first, and I think most important thing to say is, this is just an idea, and also I'm not assuming I'll take any sort of priority for thinking it up, if you like my thoughts.'

'Oh come on, just tell me the big plan.'

'Right. Well, I'm thinking we should each have a year solely looking for acting jobs while the other one gets a full-time job doing what ever brings in the most amount of money. Then the following year, the other person gets to quit the full-time job and go on the solo acting quest. What do you think?'

If Alison had said what she really thought in the first moments after Ian's suggested plan, he would have been shocked. She thought it was a stupid plan allowing, inevitably, him to look for all the best work while she supported him.

'Wow, that is a radical idea. Why now?' she said, not quite sure if her tone was derisory.

'Because we can both prosper this way. We both get a crack at something special. Theatre, telly, film, what ever comes along. And we get work experience in the so-called 'real world' with enough money to live a nice life.'

Alison sat and thought about a year without any sort of impetus or opportunity to act. Then she thought about the crappy flat they currently rented and how she wanted to live somewhere nicer. The plan wasn't so inane after all. It could work. But the big question was which of them would go first?

'All right, that does sound like a good plan. But who goes first?'

'You,' Ian said.

Alison could feel her eyebrows quickly rise in disbelief.

'Really? Why not you?'

'Because I've been offered an assistant manager's job at the bar and the money's pretty good – almost double what I'm earning now. We can get a better flat asap, and I know you're dying to tread the boards again. I had a lot of fun with the soap opera, but the bar work is actually okay. So what do you think?'

Alison smiled, then leaned across the sofa and

kissed Ian on the lips.

'I'm in, let's do it,' she said.

'Cool. So, quit the sandwich bar tomorrow and your year starts the day after you leave.'

Alison's year seemed to pass by quicker than any previous year of her life. She was aware of every day, week and month, seeing time as more precious than the oxygen in her lungs. She managed two jobs in the twelve months: Lily, the maid, in a sparsely attended short-run production of The Dead at The Young Vic; and a television commercial for personal injury claims. It was acting, she told herself on the cusp of Ian's year out; it will look good on the curriculum vitae.

'I've got a job working full time in a ticket agency. The money will cover the rent and everything we need,' Alison told Ian. Her stomach was in knots; she didn't want to go back to the dullness of a cash-on-ly-motivation career.

They added an amendment to the original plan: in the final month of their year out acting, they must secure a full-time job to make the transition seamless, so that rent, food and utilities were covered.

Ian hugged her and congratulated her again on her acting successes. She smiled, but wanted to cry.

Just over six months into Ian's year, he arrived home grinning, then humming and clicking his fingers as if he was trying to imitate jazz.

'What's happened? You've got a job, haven't you?'

'Well yes, I have got a job. You could call it a job, just a job. But I like to think of it as something a bit more than that,' he said, waggling his eyebrows and dancing Alison around the lounge.

'So, what is it?'

'Only an entire season, three sodding plays, one after the other…with the RSC at the Barbican!' Ian shouted.

His eyes were wide and his mouth was open, waiting for her to scream and leap into his arms. She hugged him tightly, forced a smile and kissed him passionately.

'That is amazing news, Ian. I'm so happy for you. How did you get the job?'

'I got a call from the RSC's casting manager. She said she'd seen me in the soap opera on a repeats channel and wondered if I fancied auditioning for the next season. I didn't want to tell you anything before I had any real news, I would have been crushed if it hadn't happened. Sorry, I hope you're not upset that I kept it quiet.'

'Of course not. It would probably have been bad luck. That's incredible news. So, three plays, the entire season. How long is that?'

'Ah, well, there's the rub.' Ian sat down and looked guilty. 'The season does run into your next year out, only by two months, but we can add those months on at the end. Is that going to be all right with you?'

Alison wanted to say no, but she knew she couldn't; he might leave her for such a golden chance, and she knew she would want exactly the same flexibility from him if she ever landed a big role.

'That's fine. You go for it. I'm so proud of you,' she said.

Ian went out to buy some Champagne and Alison

ordered a Chinese takeaway.

As she waited for him to return, she stared at her dark reflection in the television screen opposite the sofa. Her mouth was flat, her eyes daydreaming visions of utter gloom, and in the quiet of the flat, she knew she would never get her next year out acting.

As Ian went through RSC rehearsals, his pronouncements on the importance of character acting – "the real bread and butter of everything we do out there" – versus lead roles became more and more onerous, to the point where Alison, remembering Jane Pritchard's comments on character acting, found herself becoming solemn, sarcastic and bluntly rude to him.

'I get it, Ian. I did go to drama school too, remember?' she said one evening as she cleared the supper plates.

'Sorry, Al. I'm just really into this part. The Merchant of Venice is such a rich pattern of -'

'Jesus, please just shut up about fucking Shakespeare!' she shouted, dropping the plates into the kitchen sink, breaking one of them in two.

Ian's season began. He would leave every day and return to the flat as if he was going to any old job. Alison would occasionally ask if his performance went well and, most of the time, he would nod and smile, sometimes pulling a so-so face but never allowing himself to go into details. She used a free ticket he gave her and watched him deliver his lines through theatre glasses playing the servant Leonardo: "My best endeavours shall be done herein."

She did feel a huge amount of pride – he was with the RSC, an actor's dream – but she couldn't find it within herself to pass it on to him. When the three plays were completed and the season had run its course, they had a conversation that would prove to be the catalyst for the eventual end of their relationship.

'The RSC want me for the next season too, Al. But listen, wait, please. I can see what you're thinking, but I reckon we can both -'

'Another plan? I thought we agreed on equal opportunities? I am happy for you about the RSC. It's been fantastic. But the deal was a year on, then a year off. When am I supposed to find acting work?'

'You can give up that job of yours and begin auditioning whenever, that's what I'm trying to say. Listen, Al, this gig with the RSC could be a long-term meal-ticket. We can both live well and find acting jobs now. This is what we've been working for.'

Alison was jealous, completely drowning in envy. She hated feeling left behind, as if Ian was a better actor than her. He had not only achieved a lot more than she had in his first year in the acting 'workplace', but he had already reached a position she would have only ever seen after many years of grotty commercials and bit-parts.

'Fine. Okay, that sounds okay,' she said.

'Really? You're cool with all of that?' Ian said. He looked at her, squinting, as if to find some fakery in her answers.

Alison hugged and kissed him, and told him she was being irrational. They went to bed and made love. As Alison fell asleep, she thought through her behaviour and Ian's reactions in the previous couple of hours. She smiled with the knowledge that if she could fool him into thinking she was genuinely happy with the way things were – even the way she faked her orgasm – then perhaps she was a good actor, maybe better than him.

Ian became consumed with his RSC work and progressed through the ranks to bigger and better roles in the year that followed. Alison got some work: a repertory production of She Stoops to Conquer and some more, dreaded, commercials, made worse by only being broadcast online.

Her need to read reviews, find her name and see her work became an obsession as Ian's star grew larger. As she was checking one of the commercials, she decided to enter the name Nicholas Adams into the search engine.

She wasn't surprised to see film and television credits listed against his name, but was taken aback that he was listed as an assistant director.

'So you gave up acting and became your father after all,' she said to one of his Google images.

She stared into space for a while, closed her eyes and saw Nicholas all over Jane again. She crushed the memory quickly. Should she search for Jane Pritchard next? But then she saw message received on her mobile phone.

Got some amazing news. My agent says I've been offered a small part in the next James Bond film! Ian xx

Alison swallowed hard. She shut the computer down, made herself a strong cup of coffee – she added some whiskey too – and began her reply.

Alison jabbed at the letters: Great news. Are you playing Blofeld's cat?! LOL xx

Ian quickly replied: Haha, let's go out later. Love u xx

They went to an Italian restaurant to celebrate. They drank Chilean Merlot – Ian had heard it was the best – shared garlic bread and talked about his part in the upcoming film. He was playing M's personal assistant: two scenes; five lines.

Alison smiled and pretended tremendous elation for him. But her ability to perform as if her heart had been punctured with a shot of adrenalin every time he progressed was waning. She didn't like herself for the feeling, but she was sick and tired of Ian's success. She wanted him to fail, to regain the sense that he had to try as hard as she did.

'So we'll need to rent a flat near Pinewood studios. I hope that's okay?' Ian said as they walked home. 'Have you got anything coming up?'

'No. Anyway I can get the train if I need to,' Alison said, imagining life out of London: the hours of sitting and staring at the clock, waiting at home for the phone to ring; the paltry hope of offers of commercial work, anything with lines to say; and Ian bouncing in like Tigger to talk a mile-a-minute about the stunts, the car chases and, doubtless, the Bond girls.

They found a ground-floor flat near a small village. It was exactly what Alison expected: close to the studio, but a long way from London, her friends and her ambitions.

She soon found a position working part time at a company specialising in recycled products. After two weeks staring at the damned clock and telephone, checking her emails and trying to read novels she had been avoiding for years, she had made the decision that any job would do just to get out of the flat.

She met David after three days with the company. He was her boss. She began to fall in love with him almost immediately.

Where Ian had come to embody self-absorption, focused only on his own career, hardly ever asking Alison about possibilities she might be following, and seeming to have accepted her as an office-worker, David was attentive, interested and enthusiastic about her time at drama school.

They talked and laughed about anything and everything. Alison could feel her idealism for acting, for life in general, returning when ever she saw David. She began to crave her working hours.

He even offered her the lead role in a short film he was producing: the part of an amputating socio-path. He was ambitious and seemed to want to take her along with him, to raise her up to the world and tell everyone how great she was.

'Will you leave Ian if I leave Sarah?' David said one day. They were kissing in his car.

'Yes I will, yes,' she said.

After Alison told Ian she wanted to break up with him, he sat very still and stared into space.

'Why? Why now?' he asked after a few minutes. 'Things are going so well.'

'Because I've met someone else. I've fallen in love with someone else,' she said. She felt resolute, as if she were making the right decision for both of them. She had David; Ian had Bond and his precious RSC.

'And you're sure this is what you really want?' Ian said. He stood up, walked over to the sofa and sat next to Alison, holding her hand for a moment until she withdrew it.

'I wouldn't have said it if I wasn't sure, would I?' Alison couldn't resist a final blow of cruel sarcasm. She had waited a long time to give a completely honest answer to him.

Ian left the flat the following morning. There were no rages and no arguments. He returned twice when Alison was at work to collect the last of his things.

David told Sarah he was leaving her. Plans were made. Everything was set for a new future.

Alison began to remember the feeling of being at ease with herself. Her confidence in her acting, since the short film, was at a new high. She was thinking about training to become a drama teacher. Did it really matter if she became Miss Peters the way Nicholas had become his father?

Ian was gone and David was coming soon. He had been staying with his mother since leaving Sarah, although he had spent most of his nights with Alison since Ian left. He needed to sort out various legal matters and pack up his personal items, and his mother's house was closer to his previous home.

Alison was online, researching teacher-training options one morning when she felt a pain in her stomach. She ran to the toilet and vomited. Brushing her teeth to get rid of the aftertaste, she noticed an unopened packet of tampons and tried to remember when she had had her last period; it seemed like weeks and weeks. She had lost track in the break-up with Ian and planning her new life with David.

She drove to a chemist and bought a pregnancy test kit. A doctor confirmed the result two days later. The baby was Ian's.

Ben

Ben realised he was in love with Sarah the second he saw that photograph. With the use of digital technology the effect was instantaneous. It was a profile shot he had taken of her on Brighton beach, looking out to sea: a moment of quiet contemplation amidst a day of talking, music, drinking too many bottles of beer and introducing Amelia, his new girlfriend at the time. Sarah's profile was offset with a few strands of hair across her face, the sun and pier perfectly set on one side of her. She had never looked more beautiful. And he had never felt worse, knowing he had such deep feelings for his best friend's partner – David's girlfriend.

Ben met Amelia at the opening of an exhibition. She was an assistant curator. At first, he found himself drawn in by her good looks – he kept thinking of the young Audrey Hepburn – and then more deeply by her knowledge of Cartier-Bresson, Robert Capa and Diane Arbus.

'She's one of my inspirations actually,' Ben said, immediately noting a happy recognition in Amelia's face, as if she must have felt like the only Arbus fan in the world for a long time, maybe dropping her name into many conversations like this one, only to see a continual line of quizzical expressions in return.

They quickly became lovers. Ben had finally met someone he could be with, and wanted to be with, for a long time. They shared the same interest in highbrow novels and art-house cinema. They liked the same music. Amelia even taught him some new dance moves: ways of coordinating his body in time with the beat of the song, instead of the same set of wobbly legs and rolling hands he usually employed; ways that made him feel less inhibited and free to just let go.

With her easy laugh and personality that seemed so calm, and calming, he was convinced – after the debacle of false love with Stephanie and Helen, and the many one-night stands that followed – that he could emotionally breathe out and become more like the couple he most admired: David and Sarah.

That theory of lover ever after with Amelia was blown to smithereens on Brighton beach by one photograph that sent a message through his cerebral cortex and resonated with his core desire: 'It's her. It's always been her!'

Ben broke up with Amelia a week after the trip to Brighton. He felt awful. She cried and demanded to know why he was leaving her.

'I don't understand. We were getting on so well. We seemed to fit each other perfectly. What's changed?' she said.

'I don't feel that way. I'm sorry. It wouldn't be right

for me to lead you on. I can't pretend.'

Amelia stared at him in shock, her mouth open as if she was trying to speak, trying to force something out, but was too agog with a head-splitting mix of emotions so strong that she walked out of his flat, opening and slamming the door a few times as a means of final expression.

He texted David after she had left, wanting to get the news out to his best friend and treat the matter as if the whole love affair was just a big mistake and nothing to worry about. Act casual and move on.

'Come over, have a drink and we can talk like men,' David said. He had called Ben after receiving the text. They both laughed at the macho statement, but Ben knew the very last place on Earth he wanted to be was anywhere near Sarah.

'I'm going to go through my portfolio, get pissed and go to bed early, but thanks, Dave.'

As he fell asleep that night, looking at the photograph of Sarah on Brighton beach, he whispered in the darkness, 'I can't do it, Sarah. I can't let Dave down. I just can't.'

Two months went by before something happened that made Ben believe that Sarah might feel something for him too.

He had been having dinner with his two best friends, arguing with Sarah about the meaning of the word beatific, realising soon after the argument began that he was in the wrong. He was a big fan of the Beat poets and had muddled the ideas and definitions, but he was too proud of his intellect and felt too foolish to admit his errors. He found himself enjoying the level of engagement with Sarah. The total eye contact and verbal sparring seemed on the edge of something physical, and although he felt some guilt admitting this part to himself, he was enjoying excluding David.

The evening had nearly ended after the meal, when there was still an atmosphere of gentle animus. Then, as they walked past a nightclub, Sarah said she wanted to dance.

Ben expected to be sidelined after the argument, to sit with a drink and a fake grin, and watch his friends dance about in a sweaty room, but David decided to go home almost as soon as they walked into the club. Ben waved at him, happy to see him leave, found a table and bought some drinks.

After a short while of staring at other people dancing, Ben asked Sarah to join him on the floor. He didn't expect any signals of love or desire, quite the opposite after the earlier semantic cock-up. He imagined a few minutes of aimless swaying followed by Sarah telling him she was too tired to stay and would he walk her home.

But a transformation came on the dance floor. An opening and interlocking of their souls was the way he would think of the dancing later that night, as he lay in bed in a spare room across the landing from David and Sarah. They danced with each other as intimately as he thought it possible, barely touching, but even more engaged with their eyes than during the argument.

He wanted to kiss her and tell her everything he felt – he would kill and die for her – there and then. Instead he danced as if his life depended on the synchronicity of his limbs, and tried to impress his emotional connection to her with all the expressive energy his body could muster.

More weeks passed by with Ben feeling nothing but a knotted stomach of longing for Sarah. He began to avoid seeing her, meeting David in pubs to discuss their short film, and sending texts rather than phoning their landline. He was beginning to wonder if he should leave the area completely, move away and forget her – start over in a new city. He could find new subjects to photograph and perhaps finally get an exhibition organised.

He had to start making plans, because however much the dance had meant to him, however much he had felt on the precipice of all-consuming love with Sarah, nothing had actually happened during that night or after, and David was still his best friend in the world.

'So I've decided, I've finally made a decision, to leave Sarah,' David said, looking directly at Ben.

They were sitting in the lounge of the flat Ben shared with mutual friends – another couple – Richard and Kate, who were out for the evening. Ben had assumed David wanted to talk about the editing of the short film they had recently shot.

'What? Why? Dave, hang on a second, you're leaving Sarah, breaking up with her?' Ben asked. He sat forward. His voice was full of incredulity, but his heart and head were racing with sudden and far-reaching possibilities.

Ben listened to David's reasons: he had fallen in love with Alison – yes, the same Alison from the short film; he didn't feel the love and devotion he had always felt for Sarah – he loved her but wasn't in love with her; they had become companions and yet they were still so young. Now they were making wedding plans, he couldn't just coast along pretending everything would be all right.

'I have to kill my old life to create a new, and hopefully, better one. I know that sounds crass and selfish, and it is, but I won't make Sarah happy in the end. I don't think I've made her happy for a long time.'

David recounted numerous occasions from the past couple of years when he had sensed Sarah's disappointment in him and his actions. He told Ben about their bad sex, the way he had begun to see a semblance of revulsion in Sarah's eyes when they made love.

Hearing about Sarah having sex with anybody else, even David, made Ben's jaw lock in anger, but he nodded and offered the right verbal cushions to his best friend. All the time David theoretically reasoned his way out of his relationship, Ben kept thinking of ways he could have Sarah for himself. Was there a minimum time limit before he could present his love to her? What was the rule on ex-partners and best friends? Should he eventually ask David's permission?

'I'm going to tell her tomorrow. This has been eating me from the inside out for weeks. Do you think I'm doing the right thing, Ben?'

This was the moment, the one moment, when Ben could have persuaded his friend to take time to think about all the ramifications; entered a plea for Sarah that perhaps David was suffering a serious pre-wedding jitters affliction and all he needed was some distance; that he should talk to Sarah – he had nothing to lose – and really open his heart about his worries.

But as Ben studied his friend's face, he realised that this moment was actually his and not David's. David had made his choices and Ben would support him in his new life. He was sick and tired of wanting Sarah, looking at the Brighton beach photograph when he was alone and thinking about her in the abstract, as if she would only ever have been his in another lifetime.

'You should go, Dave. If you feel that strongly and things are that bad, you should go,' he said.

The next evening, Ben received a text from David saying he had told Sarah he was leaving. She had taken it reasonably well and he was already packing his things.

Ben grinned at the text, re-reading it three times. He punched the air like a victorious gladiator and looked at the Brighton beach photograph. This time his heart was beating with the energetic pulse of a man on the verge of great happiness. Perhaps the next set of Brighton beach photographs would be of Ben and Sarah holding each other, their faces pressed tightly together, smiling at the future.

He knew he would have to play things subtly now; no rushing to Sarah's side. He would keep counselling David away from his old life, keep reminding him he was making the right choices and be there for him day and night. When the time felt right, he would speak to Sarah and pray she felt the same way about him, that the dance hadn't been some kind of malevolent payback against the sadness in her relationship.

According to David, Sarah had decided to travel back to Kent to stay with her parents. It was the first weekend since they had broken up.

'She wants me out of the house as soon as possible. I can't, and won't, just be pushed out asap because it suits her. I mean, I know I made the decision and everything, but I need some time to pack and leave properly. Do you think I'm being unreasonable?' David whined down the phone line.

Ben wanted to tell his friend to just pack his possessions and get out of the house quickly, to stop punishing Sarah, and that he was being an unreasonable arsehole.

'No, that sounds reasonable enough. I guess Sarah's just feeling shocked and really upset.'

'She dumped her wedding file in the recycling bin in front of me. That was pretty fucking awful to watch.'

'Sounds it. I'm sorry, mate. This must be hard on you too.'

Ben was listening to some music in his bedroom, sipping whiskey and wondering what Sarah might be thinking and doing at her parents' home when he received a text from her, slightly cryptic in places and direct in others. She asked him to help David move out as soon as possible. And she wanted to see him to talk.

Talk about what? Did she feel she could seek him out for emotional counsel too? Did she want him to convince David to come back? There was no indication in the text that she had anything deep or meaningful to say to him.

He decided to call her home landline and leave a voice message. He was taking a chance that by not replying immediately and giving Sarah the opportunity to listen to his voice – maybe replaying the message a few times in the house on her own, gifting her the time and space to attempt to denote a specific cadence – he would be able to impart some sense of his feelings, his ardour – an old-fashioned word that encapsulated everything he was going through.

Sarah wanted the finality of her relationship brought to a speedy conclusion.

'She's got a solicitor drawing up papers,' David said. 'I receive a lump sum on the house, remortgaging or something, and then Sarah gets sole ownership. She said the meeting's on Wednesday. Everything signed and sealed, including, as she put it, the last of my shit out of the loft.'

Ben began to feel genuinely sorry for his friend; he didn't seem happy. He hadn't talked about Alison much, only confirming she had split up with her boyfriend.

In fact all he did want to talk about was Sarah and the better parts of their life together.

David had asked Ben to join him at the solicitor's office, to meet a bit before Sarah arrived. He agreed, but a couple of hours before he was due to leave he decided to send Sarah a text. He didn't want her to think he was taking sides.

He asked her if she would like to meet him for a cup of coffee. She replied she would, and they arranged a time and place – nice, simple, no complications.

Ben tried to relax. He changed his shirt three times and smoked two cigarettes, looking at his watch compulsively like a prisoner on Death Row entering the final hours of life on Earth.

When Sarah walked into the bar, Ben stood up to greet her. As soon as she sat down, his mind filled with poetic adjectives; methods of telling her he loved her; great opening lines that soon became cliché-filled. So he offered her a drink instead.

As he stood at the bar, feeling a slow trickle of sweat under one armpit, he wondered how he would ever begin a sentence to her that would eventually include the three words: I love you.

After he had distributed the drinks, nervous chatter ensued.

Eventually, Ben summoned the courage to ask Sarah about her text from Kent. What had she wanted to talk to him about? She answered, after some obvious discomfort, that she wanted to thank him for being such a brilliant friend to them both. He smiled and nodded, a pretended and modest pleasure, but he only felt a deeper sense of frustration. Was that really all she wanted to say to him?

They walked to the solicitor's office together, both of them tripping over each other's sentences, pausing to allow the other one to begin again, and generally failing to build a conversational rhythm. Ben thought this awkward melange between them was either a great sign – the shy openings of a great opera-style love affair; or a terrible portent of doom – that this meeting would essentially be two goodbyes: one for David and one for him.

Ben saw David in the waiting area, his head down, looking at his mobile phone. A receptionist asked them to sit there too. David looked annoyed and glum. Ben was late and had let his friend down, and he probably looked even more reprehensible walking in with Sarah.

He waited as David and Sarah were led away to meet with their solicitor. David had made his anger felt with some barbed comments about Ben's next photographic project, but that was to be expected and he held no grudge; David was about to sign away his home and his previous existence.

After some post-meeting discussion the three of them went back to Sarah's house to collect the last of David's boxes. Ben couldn't help feeling a kind of glee gripping his stomach when he thought of the house in that way. It was no longer the base of his two oldest and best friends; it was the home of a single woman he was in love with.

David wandered away in silence, up the stairs, to the loft. The lack of any words between him and Sarah had produced an atmosphere of subcutaneous resentment. Sarah told Ben she had finished the packing of the boxes to expedite departure matters, and knowing that made Ben wish David would just hurry the hell up and leave. He had decided to stay behind, to see David off to his new life and then just open up his emotions like arteries and let his love bleed out, hoping to make Sarah see that he was her future.

How odd it felt to be standing in such a familiar setting, waiting for your best friend to go away, so you can tell his ex-partner, the woman he was planning to marry, that you love her. Did that make him a scumbag or a romantic, he wondered.

Sarah offered Ben some tea. He said he would offer a cup to David too. It allowed him to leave the lounge and chivvy his friend along. Thankfully, David rejected the hot drink and the last of the boxes was packed into his car.

David seemed surprised but not annoyed when Ben said he was staying behind to talk to Sarah. The presumption was Ben the good guy, the listener, there for his friends in need. The two men hugged, and then David was gone.

What came next in the hours that followed when Ben went back to the house, to Sarah, was more ideal, more layered in feelings, unspoken and kept hidden for such a long time, and more emotional than anything Ben would have thought possible. After a stuttered opening, the two of them overlapping each other's words again, Ben just shut up and let Sarah say that she was in love with him.

He wasn't initially certain how to react. Should he leap to his feet? Bounce off the armchairs and sofa he had helped Sarah rearrange earlier? Or should he lead her upstairs and make love to her? She might still be feeling vulnerable and confused in the wake of David just leaving. He decided he should take things slowly; show some control.

So he brought them both a glass of water and told her he was in love with her too. He sat with her, gave her a gentle kiss and held her hand.

They ate pizza and drank some wine that evening, celebrating the advent of their new life. Ben assumed

David would be doing much the same with Alison. He didn't feel guilty or ashamed, but he knew a difficult conversation would have to be had with his friend, and sooner rather than later. He looked into Sarah's smiling eyes and wondered how anyone could start such a conversation: 'Oh, yes, by the by, after you'd gone, that very same evening, I told your ex I loved her. She loves me too and that's that, old chap. Okay with you?'

After what seemed like any and every conversational detour – first-time nerves were clearly holding them both back – Ben stood up from the dining table, kissed Sarah passionately and they went upstairs.

They kissed on the way to the bedroom. Ben thought of the Brighton beach photograph. He had always seen the image as being of someone he knew, cared for and adored, but someone he could only ever be with in his mind and stare at with love in his eyes when he held his camera up.

In the bedroom, with the curtains open and only the bedside lights on for an ambient glow, Ben began to touch Sarah's body, to kiss her neck and imagine how their naked bodies would feel locked together.

'I'm just going to the bathroom,' Sarah said, planting a long kiss on the edge of his mouth before she walked off.

Ben sat on the bed and looked around the bedroom. He had never actually set foot in there before. He had slept over in the spare room lots of times and helped David bring the boxes down from the loft earlier, which meant standing in the doorway of the main bedroom, but being in Sarah's room was another first and he was happy for that. He didn't want to retrace any emotional footsteps.

He looked at his mobile phone, on silent from earlier, half-expecting a contented message of arrival at Alison's and all's well from David, but there wasn't anything to see. He guessed his friend might be making love to his new partner and that thought made Ben feel much better. Happy endings might just be possible.

Ben was about to lie back on the bed. He glanced out of the window to his left and saw a car opposite the house that looked exactly like David's. Ben sat up and stared more intently at the vehicle. It was David's.

And David was sitting behind the wheel staring back at him.

Ben didn't know what to do. Should he drop to the floor and hope he hadn't really been seen? Commando-crawl to the back door, whisper an explanation to Sarah, and leave across various neighbours' gardens?

He couldn't move. He was transfixed, looking at David's face, which was blank of any obvious emotion: no shock, horror or raging anger.

He thought about going downstairs, giving Sarah the news, opening the front door and inviting David in to talk things through, to get the difficult conversation over and done with.

David opened the driver's door and stepped out of the car. Then he stopped. He was standing in the middle of the road, the orange glow of street lighting illuminating his face more clearly. He looked crushed by life as if he didn't have the will to take another step.

He got back into the car, turning to look up at Ben one last time.

Ben knew he had immediately transmogrified in David's mind, in that one moment, from his best friend to his worst enemy.

As Sarah came back from the bathroom and Ben watched David's car slowly drive off, he wondered if they would ever sort things out and restore their friendship or if this was the price he would have to pay for Sarah's love.

Ben smiled at Sarah, took her hand and stood up to kiss her.

He thought one more time of the sadness and defeat in David's eyes; wondered how the future would unfold. And he knew he would have to wait and see.